At Close Range

JESSICA ANDERSEN

First published in Great Britain 2007
Large Print edition 2007
Silhouette Books Limited, Eton House,
18-24 Paradise Road, Richmond, Surrey, TW9 1SR

© Dr. Jessica S. Andersen 2006

ISBN-13: 978 0 263 19866 9

Set in Times Roman 17¼ on 20 pt.
34-0707-59276

Printed and bound in Great Britain
by Antony Rowe Ltd, Chippenham, Wiltshire

JESSICA ANDERSEN

Though she's tried out professions ranging from cleaning sea lion cages to cloning glaucoma genes, from patent law to training horses, Jessica is happiest when she's combining all these interests with her first love: writing romances. These days she's delighted to be writing full-time on a farm in rural Connecticut that she shares with a small menagerie and a hero named Brian. She hopes you'll visit her at www.JessicaAndersen.com for info on upcoming books, contests and to say hi!

CAST OF CHARACTERS

Cassie Dumont—Bear Claw Crime Lab's prickly evidence specialist must defend her territory from a FBI interloper while she struggles to identify a killer. When the murderer targets Cassie, will her greatest nemesis prove to be her strongest ally?

Seth Varitek—Hampered by memories of his wife's death and his blazing attraction for Cassie, the federal evidence analyst must use all his skills to identify the murderer before it's too late.

Fitzroy O'Malley—The former Bear Claw evidence specialist retired without warning, claiming he wanted more time for fishing.

Alissa Wyatt—The crime scene analyst is one of Cassie's closest friends, but her support may not be enough this time.

Maya Cooper—The third member of the crime lab hasn't been acting like herself lately.

Bradford Croft—The kidnapper was killed months ago, yet the cases seem to be connected. Was the murderer his partner, or is there something else going on?

Nevada Barnes—Is his connection to the first crime scene enough to make him a suspect?

Denver Lyttle—Dishonourably discharged from the military, this explosives expert could be responsible for the bombs used during the kidnapping case and the current murders.

Chief Parry—Bear Claw's chief of police fears that friction between his officers and the women of the new crime lab will distract the task force.

Prologue

The hunter stalked his prey in the darkest part of the night, while the city of Bear Claw slept unsuspecting.

He cruised the streets and was soothed by the hiss of tires on salty wet pavement. He passed the shopping areas, the ski runs and the museum district. He saw that the Natural History Museum was festooned with banners announcing the upcoming grand opening of the new Anasazi exhibit, which would feature artifacts from the pueblo-dwelling Native Americans who had lived in the area long ago.

Then he turned toward one of the residential suburbs and passed a convenience store, and a darkened gas station that claimed to be open 24/7.

Moments later, trusting that the wet road had no memory of his tracks, the hunter pulled up in front of the modest split-level rental where his prey had gone to ground.

She didn't know it yet, but she was waiting for him. Had been since he'd first noticed her on the slopes, slim and sleek, handling her board like a pro, then pausing to shake out her long blond mane of hair. She was in her late teens, early twenties—young enough to have Daddy foot the bills, old enough that she slept in a basement room with a separate door to the outside, so she could come and go as she pleased.

So *he* could come and go as he pleased.

It had been three months since he last hunted, since his idiot partner had gotten too caught up in playing games with the police, too caught up in his own press. With Bradford Croft dead at the hands of the cops, the hunter had bided his time, suppressed his urges. But the changing of the seasons had heated his blood. As the predators in Bear Claw Canyon began to emerge into the spring thaw, he had emerged from his other life to hunt.

He left the engine running and the doors unlocked, fearing no thief in this suburban neighborhood. The walkway to the basement door was shoveled and salted, and wet enough that he would leave no footprint—which was important, because Croft had fallen to a footprint. The hunter wouldn't be so sloppy. He was mindful of the evidence left by his passing.

The doorknob turned easily beneath his fingertips, further evidence that she had been waiting for him. He opened the door and stepped into the carpeted room, which was steamy with too much heat. He caught a whiff of warm, female musk and his flesh hardened in response.

He craved the sexual thrill of the hunt.

There was no light from outside, and no light inside the room save for a crack of yellow brightness spilling from beneath an adjoining door. His dark vision was better than most, allowing him to detect the girl's body beneath the rumpled covers of a twin-sized cot.

He strode toward the bed, blood riding high with anticipation.

Without warning, the sliver of light snapped off and he heard motion behind the now-darkened door. He froze. Sexual excitement chilled to betrayal. The smell of female musk took on a heavier, ruttish undertone and anticipation curdled in his gut, souring to anger.

The bitch had brought someone home.

He heard the door open, heard the jingle of an unbuckled belt, the stealthy scuff of footsteps on carpet while the girl in the bed breathed deeply, unaware.

The hunter considered staying still and silent while her "date" snuck out. Indeed, the voice in his head whispered, *Stick to the plan. Make no mistakes.*

But his car was outside, running. It would be a mistake to let the lover see it. So the hunter followed the sounds of stealthy escape and let his dark-adapted eyes measure the new prey. Just under six feet, the shadow moved with a young, male swagger and the cocky arrogance he associated with professional ski bums—not the true racers, but the instructors and support staff who tried to be more than they were.

The hunter weighed his options while he slipped out of the house and eased closer to his prey on silent, rubber-soled shoes.

The ski bum weaved slightly on his feet, drunk on alcohol or sex or both, and paused beside the running car. "What the—"

The hunter closed in quickly. He struck the younger man at the base of the neck—a hard, numbing blow. Instead of falling, his prey yelled and spun, then staggered to the side and went down on one knee when the pain caught up with his booze-soaked neurons.

The hunter dropped him with a short jab to

the throat, then cursed, disappointed when the thrill drained too quickly.

Women were so much more fun.

Well, no matter. He'd take care of the ski bum and hunt again soon. Grinning at the thought, he manhandled his still-breathing prey into the backseat of the car.

"Don't worry," he told the unconscious young man, "we'll find something interesting for you. Just because you're practice doesn't mean you'll get shorted. Nothing says we can't adjust the plan."

The hunter chuckled to himself as he drove out of the quiet suburb and turned away from the city, toward the cold, lonely state parks and the empty spaces beyond. It was time to get back to work, time to let the changing seasons dictate the new phase of the plan. Soon, the Bear Claw cops would know they hadn't seen the last of the predator that had stalked them in the dead of winter.

No. The hunt was just beginning.

Chapter One

When the phone rang, FBI evidence special-ist Seth Varitek was sitting in his personal vehicle—a jade-green pickup truck with flare sides and a top-notch sports package—trying to figure out what the hell he was doing parked on the side of the highway.

This was his first weekend off in nearly a month. He should be at home, working on his long-delayed plans to turn the studio into a gym, or kicking back with a beer and a game or something. Instead, he'd found himself in the truck, headed south toward the ski areas with no intention of skiing.

He flipped open the ringing phone. "Varitek here."

"I've got a problem."

Seth instantly recognized the caller's gruff voice. Chief Parry ran the police department in Bear Claw Creek, a smallish city south of Denver, Colorado. The middle-aged man was as sturdy as a bulldog and twice as tenacious, and Seth had learned to respect him during the Canyon kidnapping case earlier in the year.

"What kind of a problem, Chief?" Even as he asked the question, Seth glanced overhead and appreciated the irony that he was parked beneath the "Welcome to Bear Claw" sign.

Damned if he knew what had drawn him back to the city two months after the kidnappings had been solved.

No, that wasn't true. He knew exactly what had drawn him, or more precisely *who*. A quick image of a long-legged blonde snapped into his head. She was all sharp angles and prickly attitude, which was just as well. He wasn't in the market for…well, for anything that was leggy, blond and irritating, that was for sure.

Which still didn't explain what he was doing in her hometown.

"I've got a murder," the chief answered. "I want your opinion on it before I reactivate the task force."

The words wiped all other thoughts out of Seth's brain and brought him upright in his seat.

When three teenage girls had been kidnapped earlier in the year, Chief Parry had set up a task force made up of his best officers, ranging from old-school homicide detectives to the three female techno-jockeys of the new Bear Claw Creek Forensics Department—BCCFD. Three weeks into the investigation, they'd asked the FBI for help and had gotten Seth's coworker out of the Denver office, Lionel Trouper.

When a series of attacks made it clear that the perp had targeted one of the forensic investigators—reconstruction and scene expert Alissa Wyatt—Trouper had called Seth to be a second set of eyes on the gathering forensic evidence.

The Bear Claw Crime Lab's in-house evidence specialist, Cassie Dumont, had taken it badly, but despite the friction—or maybe because of it—the task force had managed to find the girls, identify the kidnapper and close the case.

Or so they had thought.

Sharp interest quivered through Seth's body. "You think it's connected? How? Bradford Croft is dead."

"True," the chief answered, "but remember how he talked about 'the plan,' and how he didn't fit all of the evidence? We've kept an eye out, just in case there was a partner." Parry's voice dropped. "I'm afraid this might be proof positive. When can you get here? I've already cleared it with Trouper."

Seth glanced at the sign overhead. "As

chance would have it, I'm about five minutes from the station house. I was…" He shook his head. "Never mind. I'll see you soon."

WHEN SHE REACHED her crime scene, Cassie Dumont paused on the sidewalk and scanned the area, trying to get a feel for the neighborhood and the people.

The actual scene was inside a dingy apartment building, one of many built in the late seventies to handle the influx when the skiers discovered Bear Claw. The rear parking lot was peppered with older trucks and SUV's, most boasting four-wheel drive, a requirement for spring in Colorado. Closer to the back entrance, a pair of BCCPD vehicles and a couple of uniformed officers blocked the growing crowd.

Knowing the crowd would only get worse, Cassie pushed her way through and nodded at the uniforms. "Dumont. Crime scene."

The grim-faced men let her through, but they

didn't say anything, didn't give her an update on the situation or a "hey, how's it going?"

Their silence didn't bother her. She told herself she was used to it as she entered the dingy building.

The Bear Claw P.D. had mourned the abrupt retirement of their former evidence wizard, Fitzroy O'Malley, and they'd made life hell for the three women hired to replace him—scene specialist Alissa Wyatt, psych specialist Maya Cooper and Cassie, who worked the lab and the evidence.

Over the six months the women had been in Bear Claw, the other cops had softened toward Alissa, partly because she'd made nice, and partly because she'd hooked up with Tucker McDermott, a renegade homicide detective who seemed to have gotten partway domesticated in the past few months. But if the Bear Claw cops liked Alissa and tolerated quiet, reserved Maya because she did her work and didn't cause a stir, they had no such feelings of amnesty for Cassie.

They plain didn't like her. Maybe it was because she wasn't the sort to play nice, or because she'd shredded all of Fitz's evidence report forms—which had to be twenty years old if they were a day—and computerized the filing system. Maybe it was because she bawled out anyone who messed with her evidence, from senior detectives down to the greenest rookie. Maybe the other cops feared change. Maybe they just hated her guts. Hell, who knew?

"Who cares?" she said aloud, and the words echoed in the dreary hallway. The walls were faintly gray, as though the white paint had given up all hope of brightness, and the carpet smelled musty with years of melted snow, rock salt and other things she probably didn't want to think about. The elevator was posted with an "Out of Order" sign that was furred with dust.

"Nice place," she murmured. "Wonder if they've got vacancies."

Well, odds were they would have one soon. The chief's message had said it was a single corpse, male, presumed murdered.

The word brought a shiver to the back of Cassie's neck as she climbed the stairs to the third floor. Her imagination played tricks on her, creating the ghosts of other footfalls as though her normal partners flanked her. But Alissa was away with Tucker on very unofficial business rumored to involve a topless beach and mai tais, and Maya Cooper was off at a conference, leaving Cassie to man the crime lab alone.

That was okay. Being alone was far better than being with the wrong partner, which is what she would have gotten if she'd asked the chief for help.

Hell, look what she'd gotten during the Canyon kidnapping case, when she'd been forced to accept "help" she hadn't needed or wanted.

A faint wash of anger swept away the hallway ghosts as Cassie paused at a doorway marked with police tape. She was faintly surprised that the chief hadn't left someone at the door. Technically, he should have. But maybe it was a sign that the other cops were finally believing it when she said, "stay the hell out of my crime scene unless you have a damn good reason to be there," or "touch that and I'll break your fingers."

Alissa and Maya were always telling her to be nicer to their new coworkers, but Cassie didn't see the point. Who cared whether the other cops liked her or not? She wasn't in the job to make friends.

She was in it to do the job.

Thinking it was time to do just that, she paused for a moment to cover her shoes in a pair of oh-so-sexy paper booties she pulled from her evidence kit. She drew on powder-free gloves, snapped the lid on her kit—an orange plastic toolbox containing the basics of her trade—and breathed deeply, steeling herself for the first sight of death.

She hadn't been raised around police work. Hell, she'd started life as a chemist, and found her way into forensics after some emotional bumps and bruises. She loved the challenges of her job, the opportunity to fight for justice.

But God, she hated dead bodies.

She was always struck by the fundamental *wrongness* of a corpse, by the way her mind tried to animate the features, tried to imagine the person still breathing and moving around. No matter how many crime scenes she worked, that first moment of shock was always the same.

But the weakness was her secret. Nobody knew about it, not even Alissa and Maya.

She took another breath, told herself not to be a weenie, and then twisted the knob, opened the door and stepped inside, all in one smooth motion that didn't allow her any time to cut and run. Surprise stopped her just inside the door.

There was a man in the room, and he wasn't dead.

An impossibly large figure crouched beside a sofa bed. His wide shoulders and thick muscular legs were outlined in the dim light that filtered through a set of cheap curtains.

Between one heartbeat and the next, training kicked in. Cassie drew the weapon tucked at the small of her back and leveled it at the intruder. "Freeze! Police!"

The moment hung in the balance of friend or foe, safe or unsafe. Adrenaline was a quick shot of fight or flight, along with the knowledge that even at five-foot-ten and a hundred-thirty pounds, she was puny in comparison to this guy.

Then he turned his face into a strip of filtered light and her stomach dropped to her toes.

She jammed her weapon back in its holster. "Damn it, Varitek! What are you doing in my crime scene?"

The light from the window shadowed the FBI evidence specialist's rough-hewn features, turning his aquiline nose into a study of light and dark against the flat blades of his cheeks and the strong line of his jaw. His hair was black and buzzed, doing nothing to soften the rough edges. His eyes—pale green at the center and darker at the edges, surrounded by long, black lashes—softened the sum total of his features, but did nothing to blunt the annoyance on his face.

"Still territorial as a pit bull, I see, Officer Dumont." His voice was as dark as his looks, deep, rough and no-nonsense. He glanced up at her. "Your chief called and I happened to be in the area. You got a problem with that?"

Cassie nearly bared her teeth. Hell, yes, she had a problem. The BCCPD had its own forensics department now—there was no reason for the chief to call federal help before she was even on scene.

Not unless he thought she couldn't handle things on her own. The frustration rose to clog her throat. She'd been trying to fit in, trying to make a place for herself in the Bear Claw force by proving that she was good enough and smart enough to be one of them.

So far she hadn't made much progress, as shown by Exhibit A, who rocked back on his heels, waiting for her response.

She set her teeth. "No. I don't have a problem with you."

Varitek raised one dark eyebrow, but let the lie pass. He inclined his head toward the back wall of the single-room apartment. "What do you think?"

Until that moment, she had managed not to look at the body, had managed to block the smell of blood from her nostrils and the aura of death from her consciousness. But now she swallowed and focused on the corpse.

The young man was posed naked on a pullout sofa bed, propped up against the cushioned backrest with his legs spread-eagled beneath a white bed sheet. His arms were stretched out and his head was tipped back as though he were napping, but his chest didn't rise and fall. He was utterly still, his skin cast with a waxy, bluish sheen.

The faint burn of ligature marks at the base of his throat spoke of murder, the pose suggested a ritual. A symbol. But of what?

She glanced over at the FBI specialist. "Why did the chief call you in?" *Why didn't he wait for me to run the scene?*

Varitek rose to his feet in one powerful movement, more graceful than his bulk suggested. He topped her by a good six inches and seventy pounds or so, and she was acutely conscious of the solidity and warmth that radiated from his body. He wasn't traditionally handsome—his features were too strong for that—but when they had worked the Canyon kidnappings, attraction had flared between them, unwanted and unacknowledged.

The physical awareness hadn't faded with time apart, Cassie realized with sudden electric shock. If anything, it had gotten worse.

Unsettled, she nearly stepped back, but that

would be retreating, so she held her ground and looked up at him, waiting for an answer.

He gestured to the body. "Look at his hands."

The young man's right hand was intact, draped halfway off the sofa bed backrest. But his left hand—

"Oh, hell," Cassie breathed on a wash of shock. "The tip of his index finger is missing." She glanced at Varitek. "The chief thinks it's linked to the skeleton we found in the state park, doesn't he?"

During the Canyon kidnappings, the perp had booby-trapped a side crevice of Bear Claw Canyon and set bait for the cops. The explosion and collapse had almost killed Alissa. She had lived, but the rescuers had uncovered an older grave when they dug her out.

The skeleton had been recovered intact save for two missing bones—the skull and the first bone of one index finger were unavailable. The skull had been destroyed when the kidnapper bombed the forensics department, wiping out their new equipment and most of their bona fides within the P.D., and the finger bone had never been recovered. They assumed it had disappeared from the grave, lost to scavengers or spring runoff.

What if it had been taken instead?

Varitek said, "It's a possibility, especially given the suspicions that Croft might not have worked alone." He glanced at the body, then back to her. "Has your department made any progress on identifying the remains from the canyon?"

Cassie stiffened. "We're working on it."

Truthfully, they'd been swamped by other cases. With Bradford Croft dead and the kidnapped girls home safe, identifying the skeleton had dropped on the priority list.

Without the skull, all they had to go on was the approximate age, sex and height of the skeleton—late teens, female, around five-six—and the fact that the bones had been in the ground for a decade, give or take. Feeling a sense of empathy for the girl, Cassie had run the database searches and had come up with a handful of missing person reports in and around Bear Claw during that time period. None of them had panned out, meaning that the next step was to expand the search statewide. That'd give her a couple of hundred names, most of which—if not all—would be dead ends.

With her current caseload, Alissa's vacation and Maya's conference, Cassie hadn't found the time.

No, she corrected herself with brutal honesty. She hadn't *made* the time. So she squared her shoulders and said, "I ruled out some local missing person reports, but haven't taken it any further than that. My bad."

But Varitek didn't respond to the apology. His attention was fixed on the severed index finger. Cassie saw that a thin trail of blood had leaked onto the upholstery beneath, but the larger wound area was sealed over.

"Looks like it was cauterized premortem," Varitek said, so quietly he was nearly speaking to himself. "Souvenir, maybe?"

Disgust and a low-level horror twisted in her gut. Every now and then during the course of her work it hit her. This was real. It wasn't a movie set or a scene playing out on TV. The body belonged to a real person. Someone's son. Maybe someone's lover.

Cassie swallowed a quick bubble of nausea, while a fragment of a half remembered conversation surfaced in her brain. *Face it, you're not tough enough to hack it in the field,* Lee Adams had said. *You're a chemist, not a cop.*

Lee had been five years older than she, an instructor at the master's level forensics program she'd attended outside of Chicago. He'd been handsome and a little bit mysterious, and for a while, she'd bought into everything he said. Years later, some of his comments still snuck up on her when she least expected it.

Like now.

She set her teeth, swallowed the weakness and forced herself to think about the corpse at its most basic—as a piece of evidence in a case they'd thought was closed. "If this body is connected to the skeleton in the canyon, then Alissa was right. She did hear someone else when Croft was holding her captive. There *was* another man."

"Maybe, maybe not." Varitek stepped back so they were shoulder-to-shoulder, staring down at the body. "Don't jump to conclusions."

She felt the warmth of him and wished she didn't notice such things. He was attractive, yes, but he already had three strikes against him in her book. He was in law enforcement. He was controlling. And he was impossible to get along with. The first was a fact. The other points she'd discovered months earlier, when she'd been forced to let him into the kidnapping case and he'd taken over, brought in his own people and shoved her to the edges of the investigation, claiming she'd be safer there.

Well forget him. She wasn't looking to stay safe at the expense of the job.

She scowled. "I'm not jumping to conclusions, I'm using my version of the razor theorem—the simplest explanation is usually the correct one. We've got a body tied to a crime scene from the kidnappings. The kidnapper is dead, so we know he didn't kill this guy. Other lines of evidence have already suggested Croft had an accomplice. Ergo, we're looking at a partner."

"We're not looking at anything but the evidence," Varitek said bluntly. He turned away and reached for his bigger, meaner-looking crime-scene kit, which Cassie knew from experience contained everything hers did, and then some. He said, "Let's get to work. The sooner we release the body to the ME, the better. We're going to need a cause of death, time of death, ID…anything we can get. The chief said that based on our findings, he'll decide whether to recall the task force."

And that quickly, that easily, he took over her crime scene.

Again.

Cassie fisted her hands at her sides, so tightly that her blunt nails dug into her palms. She thought about going for her weapon. Instead, she said, "Agent Varitek?"

He didn't even turn around when he answered, "Technically, it's Special Agent."

"Yeah, you're special all right," she muttered loud enough that he could damn well hear. Then she raised her voice, but fought to keep it level. Businesslike. "Until the task force has been officially reopened and your assistance has been requested by the proper channels, I consider this my crime scene. I'd like you out of it."

"We don't always get what we want," he said, and his voice held a thread of something she couldn't quite interpret. He glanced back at her, pale green eyes unreadable. "Your boss called my boss—that's proper channels. You don't like me being here? Take it up with the chief. If you're not going to do that, then suit up. We've got a scene to work."

FOUR HOURS LATER, with the body long gone and the empty, dismal-feeling room nearly processed, Seth straightened to his full height and stretched, groaning when his joints popped in protest. His knees still ached from time to time, a legacy of his younger days when he'd gone from catcher's mitt to goalie's mask and back again, depending on the season. Not quite good enough to go pro as either, he'd slid sideways into law and then law enforcement, gotten married and then—

Irritated, he slammed the lid on that train of thought. Ancient history had no place on the job. But still, the dark memories soured his already bleak mood as he turned to make the last few notations and pack up his kit.

He was aware of Cassie watching him, aware of the tension humming between them, a mix of professional antagonism and something more complicated. She'd made it obvious that she didn't like him from the first moment they'd met. She wanted the crime scene to herself and resented his every breath. It annoyed her that he had better equipment, better contacts.

Normally, he wouldn't have wasted five minutes on a local cop who didn't want his help, but something about her drew him. Intrigued him. She was an evidence specialist who had to force herself to touch a corpse, a prickly woman with shadows of sadness in her eyes.

And those legs. He couldn't help noticing her legs. She wore tan pants cut more for field work than fashion, but they did little to disguise the long length of her calves, the sassy curve of her rear and the aggressive swagger of her hips as she moved around the room, shoulders stiff with resentment.

But even as those legs strutted through his mind, he focused on the rest of her, on the prickles, the defensiveness and the bloody-minded territoriality. All things he had no patience with, especially when they interfered with his ability to do his job.

"You ready to go?" Cassie asked. She stood near the door holding her evidence kit, which held their photographs, notes and measurements, as well as a rough sketch of the scene.

He nodded. "Sure. Let's get out of here." He hefted his own kit, which contained fiber evidence, prints and other trace samples. Ninety-some percent of the evidence—maybe even all of it—would prove useless, either unrelated to the case or too generic to be of any help.

But it was those last few percentages, those moments of discovery, that made it all worthwhile.

He just hoped to God he'd have an "aha" moment this time. He and Cassie hadn't talked about it—hell, they hadn't talked about anything—but the knowledge hung in the tense air between them.

This was no act of passion or rage, no accidental death or manslaughter. It was premeditated. Posed. Practiced.

If they didn't find this guy quickly, it was a sure bet he'd strike again.

As they left the dismal room and sealed it behind them, Seth couldn't shake the feeling that he was missing something. He didn't even try, because it was like that at every crime scene. That was part of what kept him sharp.

Cassie jerked her head toward the stairs. "I'll meet you back at the station. When I called, the chief said the task force would meet in a half hour."

Seth told himself not to watch her walk away, not to admire how her long legs ate up the hallway with an aggressive swing that was all Cassie—in a hurry and full of attitude. When she'd disappeared into the stairwell, he cast a final look back toward the sealed door, aware of something tickling the back of his brain. A connection maybe, or a suspicion.

He concentrated for a moment, but it didn't gel, so he turned for the stairs knowing the detail would surface eventually. When he reached the ground floor he saw the door swing shut, evidence of Cassie's passing. Figuring she'd left her truck in one of the visitors' slots in the back lot, he shoved open the rear exit.

And heard Cassie's voice shout, "Halt! Police!"

A weapon fired.

Then there was silence.

Chapter Two

Gun clutched in her hand, Cassie sprinted in pursuit of a dark figure nearly half a block ahead of her. She'd been stupid to shout, stupid to identify herself. Procedure be damned, she should've shot the guy the moment she saw him crouched near the back tire of her truck.

But she'd been caught up in thoughts of Varitek, thoughts of cop-shop politics. So she'd shouted and her shot had gone wide.

And now she was chasing some guy down the damn street.

Could her day get any worse?

Her lungs burned and her thighs howled, but she pushed faster. Ahead, a jean-clad figure wearing a dark ski jacket slipped on a patch of slush and went down. He scrambled up with the flexibility of a young man and skidded around a corner into a narrow street between two more crummy apartment buildings.

Cassie rounded the corner and accelerated, thinking she had the guy trapped in the alley, thinking she had—

A hot, wiry body slammed into her side, driving the breath from her lungs, sending her to the wet, cracked pavement. She screeched, tucked and rolled until she hit a steel trash bin. Then she lunged to her feet and faced her attacker.

His face was obscured by a brightly colored hat and muff combo, but she could see his eyes, which were hard, hazel chips gleaming with deadly sanity. He licked his lips. "You're a blonde. My favorite."

"Get your hands up," she ordered. "Hands up and face the wall!"

She was too slow, or he was too fast—in the moment it took her to level her weapon, he lunged and swung something glittering and metallic at her head. She ducked and the blow glanced off her shoulder. Her arm went instantly numb. She fell to the side and her gun clattered to the pavement.

The gun, she had to get the gun! She saw it under the trash bin and lunged for it just as her attacker swung again. She dodged to the side, felt road muck soak through her pants and kicked out at his ankle.

Too little, too late. He scooped up the gun, stood, turned to her—

And his eyes went beyond her, to the alleyway opening. He saluted her with her own gun, and said, "I'll be seeing you soon, beautiful." And he turned and ran.

"Cassie!" Varitek pounded up to her, grabbed her arms and dragged her to her feet. "Are you hurt?"

"Let go of me!" She tried to shake him off but he wouldn't shake, so she kicked at him. "He's getting away!"

But Varitek was as immovable as granite. He held onto her with one hand and waved as two panting uniformed officers ran past. "He went out the back. About five-ten, male, jeans and a dark jacket. Red hat."

As the officers bolted past, Cassie recognized the men who'd been watching the rear exit when she'd entered the crime-scene building. But where the hell had they been when red hat was messing with her truck?

When Varitek's grip on her arm slackened, she yanked away. Then she got in his face and poked him in the chest. "Why didn't you chase him? I was fine!"

At the moment her brain reported the feel of his rock-hard chest beneath her fingertip, he seemed to grow bigger, looming over her, dark brows furrowed, light green eyes nearly shooting sparks. "You were *not* fine! The bastard knocked you down and roughed you up. And where the hell's your gun?" When she didn't answer, he cursed. "He got it. Great.

Nothing like paperwork to round out the night, never mind the idea of arming another criminal."

She refused to back away, refused to back down even when the angry heat radiating from his body snuck through the chilled layers of shock and set up a vibration in her core. She held onto her anger when a sneaky little voice tried to tell her that he was right, maybe she should've waited for backup.

"What's your problem?" she snapped. "I'm a cop just like you. Hell, I've probably got more street time logged in the past few years and I can bloody well handle myself. Don't you get it? I'm not your problem!"

In a flash, he grabbed her by the front of her jacket and lifted her clean off her feet to press her against the rough wall of a nearby apartment building. Her heart jammed into her throat at the physical shock of his strength and his nearness.

She started to struggle, to curse him, to knee

him where it hurt if that was what it took, but
the look in his eyes stopped her. There was no
rage, no irritation, not even a hint of the heat
she'd seen moments before.

There was nothing. Complete, utter blankness.

"Have you ever seen a dead woman in an
alley covered with her own blood?" he asked,
and his voice sounded as though it was being
ripped out of him. "Have you ever gotten there
just in time to hear her last words, her last
breath?" There was something in his eyes,
something bleak that tore at Cassie even as fear
quivered in her chest. She started to answer, but
he cut her off with a shake. "I have," he choked
out. "I know how it feels, damn it! I…"

He broke off and abruptly released his hold
on her jacket, dropping her to the ground. He
stood there, looking down at her for a moment,
and the pain was gone from his eyes, leaving
only a cool, pale green stare.

"Varitek?" she said, her brain grappling with
what had just happened. When he didn't

respond, she drew breath to demand an explanation, a response, anything, but before she
could speak, a siren's whoop drew their attention and a BCCPD four-wheel drive vehicle
nosed into the narrow street.

Chief Parry emerged. "You two okay?" he
asked, eyes cutting between them with
piercing intensity.

"We're good," Varitek answered in his trade-
mark deep voice, showing no evidence of what
had just happened between them. "Did you get
the guy?"

"No," Parry replied, disgust written plain on
his weathered features. "Damn it all. He
dumped the hat and the jacket and blended."

"I'll want the clothing," Varitek said, not
even bothering to glance at Cassie. "It'll give
us DNA at the very least. You never know.
Punk like that might pop up in one of the databanks."

Feeling excluded and angry, Cassie stepped
forward. "What did he do to my truck?"

The men stared at her, reminding her that she'd been the only one to see the dark figure crouched down by her tire. She quickly sketched in the events leading up to the chase.

The more she talked, the harder Varitek scowled. He shot a glance at the chief, who nodded and said, "I'll get the bomb squad boys on it."

A quick shiver of fear reminded Cassie that they had never actually connected Bradford Croft to the bombings during the kidnapping case. Though he'd checked into a few Web reference sites on explosives, he had no formal training, and their bomb expert, Sawyer, had deemed two of the devices fairly sophisticated.

"You two coming?" the chief called, indicating his vehicle.

Varitek nodded for Cassie to precede him, but once ahead, she turned to face him, stalling them out of Parry's earshot. "What the hell happened back there?"

He didn't pretend to misunderstand, just

growled, "Nothing you need to know about. It won't happen again." Then he brushed past her, climbed into the SUV and yanked the door shut with a final slam that sounded gunshot-loud.

Conversation closed.

CASSIE'S QUESTION reverberated in Seth's head an hour later as Chief Parry stood at the front of a BCCPD conference room and walked through a summary of the Canyon kidnappings.

What the hell *had* happened back there?

A flashback, maybe, or a memory. He didn't know. Whatever it was, he'd suddenly been back in a different, darker alley while a brown-haired woman bled out in his arms. Her eyes had focused on his face just before she died.

The thought of it, the guilt and the rage of it, closed a fist around his heart.

"The evidence showed that Bradford Croft killed his mother," Chief Parry said, drawing Seth's attention out of the past, to the current case, which refused to behave cleanly. The chief said, "And he admitted his guilt of the kidnappings to Officer Wyatt. However, he died of his injuries before we were able to clear up a number of discrepancies, including his original alibis, which collapsed under scrutiny, and whether the skeleton found at the scene of the first explosion was tied to the case."

"Which makes all this pretty darned speculative," Tracy Mendoza interrupted, then tacked on a belated, "Sir." When the chief nodded for her to continue, the homicide detective said, "The missing finger seems to connect the older skeleton with today's murder, but our only evidence tying the skeleton to the kidnappings is location. It could be a coincidence."

The chief nodded. "That's possible, but we're not ruling out anything until the evidence tells us to. Until that time, we'll remain open to the possibility that the older skeleton is connected to today's body and both

are related to the Canyon kidnappings."
Parry's eyes hardened to flint. "There's a
murderer on the loose in Bear Claw. Let's get
him."

He got nods and murmurs of agreement until
Mendoza's partner, an older, harder detective
named Piedmont, said, "It would've helped if
the crime lab had reconstructed the old skull."
He curled his lip at Cassie, who was sitting
alone at the far edge of the room, over near the
wall. "Too bad they lost it."

Cassie shot to her feet and snarled at
Piedmont. "We didn't lose the skull. The kidnapper blew it up along with my lab. And let's
not forget that it was your sloppy security that
let the guy into the police department in the
first place."

The Bear Claw cops grumbled, but she had
a point. The forensics lab was located in the
basement of the P.D. Nobody should have
been able to walk in past the front desk and
make it to the stairs without authorization.

Nobody but a cop, Seth had thought at the time, but none of the other evidence backed up that possibility.

At least none that they'd found.

Chief Parry stepped in before the grumbles could degenerate. He raised his hands. "Okay, here's how it's going to work. I'm breaking the task force up into three teams. Team one is going to investigate the canyon skeleton. Use the ME's notes and whatever forensics can tell you and go from there. Team two is going to work the new murder. Team three, composed of the forensics department and Special Agent Varitek, will act in a support capacity for the other teams."

The chief read off the names on teams one and two, but before he could dismiss the task force, Seth stood, knowing there was one thing left to say, knowing it wouldn't make him popular. "Chief? May I have a moment?"

Parry acknowledged him. "Of course."

Seth cleared his throat. "We need to

consider one more aspect of this—the safety of our officers, particularly the women." Saying it aloud brought the dark memories closer. "I'm not trying to be sexist here—" well, maybe he was, but he had a damn good reason for it "—but don't forget what happened during the kidnappings. Croft focused his attentions on Alissa Wyatt and nearly killed her. If this is connected, then the pattern could repeat."

Cassie frowned and spoke up. "If it's connected, then he's already broken pattern. All the other victims, including the skeleton, were women under twenty. The murder victim was a man in his mid-twenties."

Seth countered, "The bomb squad didn't find any charges under your truck, but the brake lines were severed and reconnected with a thermolabile polymer." Anger flared in his chest at the thought, and at the fact that she didn't seem nearly worried enough. The lines would've given out with heat and use—like once she was on the highway, or maybe one of the mountain roads. "Face it. You're already a target."

She lifted her chin and stared him down. "Don't try to protect me. I can take care of myself."

The words echoed through memory to another woman, another time. Seth growled, stepped around the podium and—

"Thank you, Special Agent Varitek." The chief got between them and diverted Seth to his chair with a warning look. "Based on that evidence, I think we need to assume that the female officers are at higher risk, and Officer Dumont in particular." He scanned the room and made two partner changes, breaking up a pair of male detectives and a pair of female detectives and switching them. "That leaves everyone protected except Officer Dumont." The chief looked at Seth. "You'll keep an eye on her?"

"Yeah," Seth said, though he wished there was another option. "I'll watch her back."

At that, Cassie shot to her feet and stalked from the room, shoulders tight, body language just this side of aggressive.

The door slammed behind her.

CASSIE POUNDED DOWN to the basement crime lab, nearly vibrating with fury.

Maybe she should be used to being under-estimated by now, but it still stung. How long would she have to fight the fragile female ste-reotype? How many heads did she have to bite off, how many testosterone-laden men was she going to have to chase away from her ter-ritory before they'd believe that she was smart enough, tough enough and street-savvy enough to do the job she'd been hired to do?

In all honesty, Varitek probably wasn't trying to be a jerk. There was some logic to his words. It had been a tense, ugly situation when Croft had targeted Alissa. But she wasn't Alissa, and this wasn't the same situation. Cassie couldn't afford to be coddled, and she'd be damned if he shoved her to the side of another investigation.

She glared around the lab, part of her wishing for someone to fight with, part of her glad to be alone in the one space that made her feel truly welcome. The banks of machines didn't care what she looked like or whether she peed sitting down. They answered the questions she asked, using the information she gave them. She could load in two DNA samples and be confident that the next morning, the fluorescent peaks and valleys on the computer printout would tell her whether she had a match or not. Whether she had a mixed sample or not.

The evidence didn't care who she was.

She let her fingertips drift over the stereomicroscope she used to examine fiber, hair and dirt samples. She glanced at the logged evidence from the apartment murder scene, the jacket and hat from the bastard who'd rigged her truck. But though she was tempted to dive in, she knew better.

She was too ticked off to work effectively, too distracted. Her thoughts were jammed with Seth Varitek. She was all tangled up with the sound of his deep, masculine voice, and the feel of being pressed up against the wall of a crummy apartment building. He'd invaded her senses until she swore she could taste him on her lips, which was impossible.

Cursing, she strode out of the lab and into her small office, where she threw herself into her desk chair and slapped her computer mouse to wake the machine from its screen saver.

Then she stared blankly at the glowing icons.

"Stop taking this so personally," she said aloud, hoping the words would help put the scene upstairs into perspective. "He wasn't saying you couldn't take care of yourself. He was just saying to watch out."

Only he'd said more than that. He'd agreed to "watch her back," which she translated as "keep her in the lab while I work the field." He was an excellent evidence tech, but so was she. And she was the one who'd be staying in Bear Claw once this was over. *She* was the one who lost status in her coworkers' eyes every time she let the FBI take over a crime scene.

She lost. Not him.

So, yeah, it was personal. Maybe not to him, but it sure as hell was to her. With Alissa and Maya out of town, it was up to her to defend the value of the new forensics department. It was up to her to make herself indispensable to the BCCPD, so the other cops would finally realize that she was worth something to the department.

That she was worth something at all.

Lee's voice whispered around the edges of her mind, telling her it wasn't enough, that it would never be enough. Gritting her teeth against a press of anger, she clicked over to her favorite Web search engine. She typed two words into the query box.

Seth Varitek.

If this was going to be a battle for control of the Bear Claw Forensics Department, it made sense for her to know her enemy, to know his weak spots, if there were any. And though public records might not give her the insight she needed, the Web was a good place to start. She didn't need to be a full detective to know that.

She avoided his public profile on the FBI field office Web site. She'd checked it out a few weeks after he'd left Bear Claw, just out of curiosity, and had been unsettled by the hot rush that had punched through her when she'd seen his official photo. In the picture, his dark hair was buzzed close to his skull and his pale green eyes seemed to stare directly at her. It was by no means a glamor shot, it was too rugged for that, too fierce. But it had encapsulated what she remembered of the man, and it had left her far warmer than she'd liked.

"So we'll skip that site," she muttered to herself. "We'll stipulate that he's relatively hot and move on to the important stuff—figuring out what makes him tick."

She kept one eye on the door as she clicked through lists of the papers he'd authored in recent years. He'd come looking for her sooner or later—to gloat if nothing else—and it wouldn't do for him to find her prying. Wouldn't do for him to know that she was interested, if only in the context of defending her territory.

The search results were sorted by date, so it took her ten minutes or so to work through the past couple of years' worth of information on Varitek, mostly notations of meetings he'd attended or spoken at, research he'd done on computer simulation models and methods for integrating the various criminology databases.

"No wonder he has all those cutting-edge programs to work with," she said, impressed in spite of herself. "He developed some of them."

That also explained why he was a general-ized evidence guru when so many of the FBI forensics experts specialized in one field, whether it be hair or paint chips or DNA. But that didn't really help her. She needed something more. Something personal. Then she clicked on the next screen worth of information and hit pay dirt.

Only it wasn't the sort of dirt she'd wanted to find.

It was far worse.

The newspaper articles were from the major Denver papers. The headlines jumped out at her, highlighted one-line summaries that told a terrible story.

She sucked in a breath and moved to blank the screen, but a hint of movement and a low curse from the doorway warned that she was already too late. She spun in her chair and saw that Varitek stood in the doorway of her small office, close enough to read the damning words over her shoulder.

His eyes were dark, his expression closed. "Find what you needed, Officer?"

Her stomach knotted and she stood, unwilling to let him loom over her. "I'm sorry. I shouldn't have pried."

He didn't nod, didn't smile, didn't let her off the hook. Instead, he said, "No, you shouldn't have. It's none of your business." He didn't move, didn't even seem to be breathing, though she knew that was an illusion. "How much did you read?"

"Not much," she answered quickly. "Just the headlines."

Headlines like *Woman Murdered Returning Home From Art Show,* and *Cop Husband Vows Revenge Against Diablo Brothers.*

"Then what else do you want to know?" he said, voice dark with an emotion that didn't show in his face. "Should I tell you that Robyn and I fought about that damned art show? She wanted people to know how run-down the schools were in that section of town, wanted to help improve them. She moved her paintings down there and planned a party, a grand opening for God's sake." Grief deepened the lines beside his mouth and the muscles at his jaw bunched with tension. "I made her promise not to go out there without me. Then I let her down because I got a call. A break in the case." He paused. "It was a plant, of course. A diversion. I got back just in time to find her. In time to say goodbye."

Cassie made a wordless sound of sympathy while her heart tore in her chest and leaked pain. She reached out, but didn't quite touch him. "I'm sorry."

The words seemed inadequate. She reached over and blanked the computer screen, as though erasing the headlines could erase the memories.

"If I'd been there to drive her home…" His expression was closed, as though he were talking to himself now, as though this were a conversation he'd been through a thousand times in his head. "If I'd been better about sep-arating my life from my work…" He trailed off and refocused on her. He scowled, but the expression didn't seem as fierce as it had before. "Sorry. Not your problem."

But it *was* her problem, she realized. It explained what had happened back in the alley, and why he had moments of being as overprotective as one of her four older brothers. Why he kept trying to push her to the edges of her own investigations.

It was her problem, because it was affecting her ability to do her job and make her place in Bear Claw.

Knowing it, but also knowing that she'd never been good at touchy-feely emotional conversations, she jammed her hands into her pockets. "I'm sorry, Varitek. There's nothing I can say to make it better. Nothing at all. But I won't let you shut me out of this case like you did with the kidnappings, just because I'm a woman and you're afraid I might get hurt."

He scowled down at her. "I didn't shut you out."

He was closer than she'd realized, a mere half step away. She wanted to retreat from the warmth of him, the sheer size of him, but held firm. "Yes, you did. Maybe you didn't mean to, and maybe the lab fire made it simpler to use FBI equipment and personnel. But in the end, it was your work, not mine, and everyone here knew it."

"I didn't—"

She held up a hand to stop him. "Don't worry. We're both at fault because I let you take over. But not this time. This time you're on my turf and I'm not giving it up." She took a breath. "Look, I'll admit it. With Alissa and Maya away, I could use help. But this is going to have to be *my* investigation and *my* evidence collection. I'm in charge this time."

She expected an explosion, but instead he closed the scant distance between them, until that damn warmth kindled in her midsection and she saw the heat reflected in his eyes. "What do I get if I agree?"

Her first thought was so thoroughly sexual that she stumbled back on a wash of heat and surprise before catching herself and standing fast. Since when did her mind dwell in the gutter?

Sure she'd been on a dating hiatus for the past few months while getting settled in Bear Claw, and before that she'd stuck to casual things that rarely developed past pleasant kisses. She liked sex well enough, but she'd been…busy. Why had her body picked *now* to wake up?

She gritted her teeth, forced the heat aside and said, "What do you want?"

He stared down at her for a moment, and she didn't dare interpret his expression, which was part closed off, part something else. Then he said, "The guy in the alley said he'd see you again. If he wasn't focused on you before, he is now."

The chilly logic chased away some of the heat. Cassie crossed her arms and swallowed a bubble of worry. "That's good. It'll give us something to work with. Maybe he'll be stupid and make a mistake."

"And maybe he won't," Varitek countered, voice dead level. "Bradford Croft wasn't as smart as his crimes. That, plus the murder scene today, tells me we're dealing with the slicker of the partners. We can't count on him making a mistake."

Cassie forced herself to meet Varitek's eyes. "Which means?"

"That you're in danger," he answered flatly. "So here's the deal. I'll let you run the case and make you look good in front of the locals, but I'm in charge of security. In the lab, in the field, wherever. No debates, no questions asked. What I say goes."

She bristled. "You're not *letting* me do anything, and I don't need you to make me look good."

"Take it or leave it." He shrugged. "I'm not here for a turf war. I'm here to help you people find a murderer before he strikes again." His eyes sharpened on hers. "And he *will* strike again. Soon."

She couldn't argue against that. The pose and the missing fingertip argued for ritual. The lack of good evidence argued for the perfection of long practice.

Yes, the killer's appetite would be whetted now. It was only a matter of time.

But it galled her to give Varitek control. She didn't need anyone to protect her. She could take care of herself. Hadn't she proved that when she moved away from her father and her four too-protective older brothers?

That thought brought an insidiously undermining voice that said, *Yes, and you hooked up with a man just like them, only much, much worse.*

"Do we have a deal?" Varitek asked, snapping her away from the memory of being weak.

She stiffened her spine because she wasn't weak anymore, damn it. But she also wasn't stupid or suicidal. Varitek had a point, whether she liked it or not. The guy in the red hat had rigged her brakes, and he'd promised to see her again.

So finally, though she wished there was another option, she nodded. "Deal."

They didn't shake on the agreement. She told herself it was because they didn't need to, that their words were good enough. But deep down inside, she knew why she didn't offer to shake his hand.

She didn't want to know what it would feel like to touch him. Rather, she wanted it too much, and physical attraction had been her downfall once before.

She wouldn't let that happen again.

Chapter Three

The next morning dawned a balmy forty degrees, which was both good and bad news for Cassie and Seth, who had decided to reexcavate the canyon gravesite in search of additional clues. It was good news because the ground would soften up quickly. Bad news because it meant they would be working in mud.

Knowing it, Seth skipped his usual slacks and button-down shirt and went with jeans and a sweatshirt. He kept a packed overnight bag in his truck, which saved him from having to hit the local mall. He armed himself with the backup weapons he kept in the truck's locked console, and pulled out of the hotel parking lot feeling more centered than he had the previous day.

He'd considered spending the night on Cassie's couch, but she'd nixed the plan in no uncertain terms and he hadn't pushed because he'd needed the time away from her, needed to decompress.

He'd worked hard to deal with the memories and the guilt, yet a few old headlines on a Web search engine had slammed him right back to that place, breaching his defenses and sweeping him into the memories before he'd been prepared.

Seth braked the truck beneath a red light, and scrubbed a hand across his face, though that did nothing to erase the image of a delicate, dark-skinned woman with a riot of curls and laughing brown eyes. Robyn. Sweet, big-hearted, impulsive Robyn. They had met in college and immediately embarked upon a tumultuous relationship. The sex had been fantastic, their friendship less so, but that hadn't seemed to matter. They broke up, got back together, broke up again and got back together again just after Seth entered the FBI.

That time it had stuck. They had married a year later, and if marriage hadn't ended their problems, it had given them a moral and legal imperative to stick it out. Seth didn't believe in divorce. Hell, his parents had been together going on forty years. They'd taught their children—Seth and his older sister, CeeCee— that marriage was a forever thing. Choose it once and don't falter.

Well, Seth had tried not to falter, but he had in the end.

An annoyed horn blast warned him that the light had gone green, and Seth hit the gas, angry at himself for going down that mental path when he had more relevant things to worry about.

Like catching a killer while protecting an evidence tech who didn't want to be protected.

He'd asked the chief to send patrols past

Cassie's house at intervals throughout the night. They hadn't reported anything suspicious—Seth had checked—but he didn't relax until he arrived at the neat, two-family house she'd sublet.

She answered the door at his knock, wearing jeans and a sweatshirt akin to his, along with a battered-looking parka and lace-up boots with a sturdy tread. Her glossy blond hair was pulled back in a severe ponytail that accented the graceful sweep of her neck. His eyes locked onto the soft spot behind her ear, and the ragged frustrations of a long, sleepless night redirected themselves into an unfamiliar sizzle.

An unexpected want.

She glanced over at him and her brows drew together. "You ready?"

That was the question, Seth realized. He was ready for the case, but not for her. He wasn't ready for the way his blood kicked when he saw her, the way he seemed to have already memorized her features, and the way he noticed how she always took a deep breath before turning on the attitude, as though it wasn't entirely natural for her.

That was why he'd driven to Bear Claw in the first place, he finally acknowledged. To test himself. To tempt himself.

When he and Cassie has worked together earlier in the year, sparks had flown as they'd clashed over everything from fingerprinting techniques to lunch orders. At first that had been a relief, because he'd promised himself that when it was time to date casually again, he'd choose women he got along with rather than the ones who stirred him up. But once he'd returned to Denver, he'd found himself thinking about her, wondering how she was doing and who she was doing it with.

Bad sign.

"Yeah, I'm ready. Let's go." He stepped back from the door and gestured to his truck.

The sooner they got digging, the sooner he

could get back to Denver with his question answered. Maybe he was ready to emerge from the isolation of the past four years and date again. But there was no way he was ready— or willing—to date Cassie Dumont. He wanted a calm, mature friendship with a woman, something based in common ground this time, rather than attraction and excitement.

The decision should have made him feel better as they walked to his truck in silence, then drove out to the state forest.

So why was he more frustrated than ever?

He didn't have an answer for that as he turned his truck into the Bear Claw Canyon State Park, bypassed the parking area and followed a narrow track into the park, almost to the edge of Bear Claw Canyon.

When they'd both climbed out of the truck and shouldered their equipment, Cassie glanced sideways at him. "You okay?"

"I have a bad feeling about this case," he said, not really answering the question.

She bristled. "If you'd bothered to let me help before, you'd know that I'm damn good at my—"

"I'm not talking about your work!" he snapped. "I'm talking about your truck brakes and the guy in the red hat, about the fact that you're in—" He cut himself off, snapping his jaw shut on the words because he already knew they wouldn't do any good. Cassie was on a mission to prove herself to the other cops, and there was no way in hell she was letting him win this argument.

Just like Robyn and her damned art show.

Cassie stepped closer, so close he could smell the faintest hint of woman over the earthy scent of the spring thaw. That fragrance tangled itself in his soul, where Robyn and Cassie had somehow gotten mixed up together. She said, "Look, Varitek. My mother died when I was a little girl, but I've never lost someone close to me as an adult. I won't pretend to know how it feels. I can't. But stop trying to put your past on me. I'm a cop. Either you find a way to treat me like one or this isn't going to work."

"That's—" *ridiculous,* he started to say, but couldn't because they both knew she had a point. He wasn't treating her like a cop. Hell, he wasn't even treating her like the female agents and officers he dealt with on a daily basis. He was treating her like…what? A girl-friend? A lover?

She was neither.

So he inclined his head and stepped back, letting himself be the one to back down this time. "Fine. You're a cop. Let's dig."

THEY WORKED IN PARALLEL, setting up portable heaters to melt through what was left of the slushy spring freeze, and clearing away the mud layers they'd backfilled after the original excavation of the grave. There was no conver-sation, no banter between coworkers.

At first, Cassie was grateful for the silence,

which gave her time to settle down. After a while, she even admitted—to herself at least—that Varitek wasn't the only one at fault. No matter what he said or did, her first response was to attack. Maya had commented on it during the earlier case, but Cassie had brushed it off as Maya being Maya. The psych specialist didn't know when to turn it off and stop analyzing people.

But now, soothed by the rhythm of digging, Cassie forced herself to take a good hard look at her behavior over the past day. Heck, the past six months, ever since the three women had moved to Bear Claw and set up the new department.

The best defense is a good offense, her father always said. A man's man, Cody Dumont had been far more comfortable with aphorisms and sports metaphors than one-on-one conversations. But was he right?

Even Alissa had suggested she tone down the attitude, and that wasn't Alissa's style. As

Cassie dug down to the farthest reaches of the original excavation and resieved the muddy slime for a bone or bullet fragment they might have missed, she wondered whether her friends had a point.

It wasn't Varitek's fault she didn't fit in. It was hers. Maybe Lee had been right, after all. Maybe she couldn't cut it.

At the thought, she heard the clatter of something distinctly unmudlike in her sieve. "Hey! I've got something!"

Varitek was at her side in an instant. "Bone?"

"No. Metal. Jewelry, maybe?" Professional excitement buzzed through her as she worked the object free of the clingy, frozen earth, careful to set aside the surrounding material for further analysis. "A ring, I think."

Sure enough, once she rinsed it in the bucket of water she'd set aside for the purpose, she caught the glint of yellow gold and the flash of a fat red stone.

Varitek squinted at it. "A class ring, I think.

Should be traceable." He grinned at her and nodded. "Good work."

The two words shouldn't have warmed her so thoroughly. She told herself it was professional pleasure that he'd credited her with the discovery, cop-to-cop.

She almost believed it.

She photographed, bagged and tagged the evidence, then stowed it in her kit to take back to the lab.

They wouldn't expect to get any trace evidence off it—previous testing of the strata and bones had indicated that the skeleton had been in the ground for ten to fifteen years— but if they were lucky, it would help them identify the remains.

And from there, maybe the killer.

"Want to keep going?" Varitek asked.

She rocked back on her heels and surveyed the scene. "Well, we've gone down to the original excavation and past it by about six inches. We're in undisturbed ground for the most part, so we probably won't find anything else. That being the case, let's go down another two inches just to be sure."

He nodded. "Works for me." He glanced at the sky, which was clear and bright with spring. "The weather's on our side, and putting a name to this skeleton would be a huge break." He dug in. "Besides, the next task force meeting isn't until this evening."

The chief had timed their meetings for the overlap when the day shift went off and the night shift was just coming on. It sounded good in theory, but in practice the task force cops worked pretty much round the clock and reported in when they had something.

Knowing it, Cassie kept one ear out for the ring of her cell as she and Varitek skimmed off another layer of wet grit.

The first call was from the ME, Boniface, who reported that the young man had died of strangulation, as the ligature marks had suggested, and that the finger wound had likely been caused by a smooth bladed knife. He couldn't explain the cautery of the wound, but theorized that the knife could have been heated.

Cassie made a mental note to check the wound scrapings for carbonization that might support the hypothesis.

Other reports filtered in as the afternoon grew long and the grave widened. Mendoza and Piedmont reported that the apartment where the body was dumped had been rented six months earlier in the name of Randy Meyers, but things got complicated after that. Meyers, a midlevel extreme skier, had been tracked down in Tahoe. He claimed to have handed the apartment over to a female friend when he'd grown bored of the Bear Claw slopes. She, in turn, had sublet to some guy, first name Nevada, last name unknown.

They would identify the body eventually, but it would take time.

After that report, there was a lull in the phone traffic and the silence hung heavy.

Finally, almost unwillingly, Varitek said, "You mentioned that your mother died when you were young. That must have been tough."

Cassie wasn't sure which surprised her most, that he'd made a personal comment, or that he remembered her passing mention. Then again, they were up to their elbows in a grave. Death seemed like a reasonable topic.

"My father raised me from five on," she answered, "and my four older brothers pitched in. They nearly smothered me with their good intentions, but I love them dearly." She paused, then added, "From a distance."

Varitek smiled slightly. The expression softened his face just enough to take it from fierce to unexpectedly sexy. "I have an older sister," he said. "CeeCee was overprotective as hell when we were kids. I can't begin to imagine what four brothers must've been like."

"A little like you times four," she said without thinking, disarmed by the fact that they were actually having a pleasant conversation, "only they don't have the tall, dark and handsome thing going for them."

Then she froze. *Oh, God. Please tell me I didn't just say that aloud.*

But his sudden, complete stillness told her that she had, indeed.

She climbed to her feet, stripped off her gloves and faced him. Blood tingled in her cheeks. "Sorry. That was uncalled for, especially after I lectured you about treating me like a cop. Let's forget I said that. Let's forget I even thought it."

But when Varitek stood and faced her, his expression was intent and wholly focused on her. "You want to know why I reached the crime scene before you yesterday? Because I was already in town. I'd driven down here for no real reason except to drop in on you and see…" He twisted his lips with more self-deprecation than humor. "Hell, I don't know why. Because I couldn't get you out of my head, I suppose."

Blood skimmed through her body, just below her skin, warming her, worrying her. She blew out a breath and said, "Look, Varitek—"

"You should probably call me Seth at this point, don't you think?"

"Look," she said, and skipped the name entirely, "this is a really, really bad idea. We can barely hold a civil conversation, and I'm not in the market for a... whatever." She'd been uncomfortable talking about her emotions ever since her relationship with Lee, who had been a master of taking those emotions and turning them back on her until she wasn't sure where her opinion left off and his began. Besides, she wasn't about to name the things that flitted through her mind, like...lover. Boyfriend. Husband. Soulmate.

"I'm not in the market for a whatever, either." A dark, introspective smile touched his lips. "I think maybe that's why I came down. So I could remind myself that we'd be wrong together."

"We'd be terrible," she said, as much to herself as to him. "I'm cranky and territorial. You're controlling and overprotective. Hell, we don't even work well together." Although they had excavated the grave shoulder-to-shoulder and it hadn't been as awful as she'd feared. Indeed, it had been almost…solid. Good. She felt the hard bump of the class ring folded in its plastic envelope and knew they'd made progress.

But she'd let physical attraction override common sense once before and it had been a disaster. Hell, it'd nearly ruined her career. No way she was letting that happen again.

She was older and smarter now.

Wasn't she?

HOURS LATER, after they'd attended the task force meeting and logged in the evidence from the old gravesite, Cassie finally signed out and headed home. With her truck impounded as evidence—wasn't that ironic?—she had no wheels, so she didn't even bother with a token protest when Varitek offered to drive her home.

She bristled when he walked her to the door.

Key in hand, she faced him on the front porch. "I'm not asking you in."

The corners of his mouth twitched. "I didn't expect you to. I'll stay out here while you check the house."

"Go." She waved him off with a shooing motion, too tired to deal with him. "I'll be fine." When he didn't budge, she said, "Come on, give me a break here. I'm tired, I'm hungry, and I'm armed. Just go. I'll see you in the morning."

After a momentary stand off, Varitek scowled. "Fine. See you tomorrow." He stalked away, leaving her feeling like she'd been childish and surly.

Which she had been.

"Oh, fine," she muttered under her breath, stabbing her key into the lock. "I'll apologize to him tomorrow." She twisted the knob and pushed through the front door as Varitek's truck pulled away.

Two steps inside her door, someone grabbed her. She screamed and tried to spin, but he yanked her arm up behind her back. The sharp pain of a needle flared in her shoulder, followed by cool, burning numbness.

Then nothing.

SETH MADE IT ALL THE WAY to his hotel before he turned back. He told himself not to bother, that they could talk it out in the morning when one—or both of them—was in a better frame of mind. But something compelled him to spin the truck around and head back to her yellow house on the outskirts of town.

When he got there, he saw that the other half of the side-by-side two-family was lit. A shadow skimmed past a curtained window as he watched. The neighbors were still up. In contrast, all of the lights on Cassie's side of the house were off—not just the outside light that had been burning when he'd left, but the room lights, as well. It was as though she'd never come home.

She's asleep, he told himself, though it wasn't much past eight o'clock. *She skipped dinner and headed straight to bed.*

Then he saw the barest hint of motion at the corner of the house, near Cassie's side window. It could've been a small animal in search of scraps.

It could've been an intruder.

Seth slapped the truck into Park, radioed an alert to the Bear Claw dispatcher, grabbed his flashlight and service revolver and hastened across the muddy lawn. He didn't even think about chasing the shadow. He needed to get to Cassie first, needed to know she was okay.

And if that meant he was ruled by his past, then so be it.

He crossed the porch in three echoing strides and pounded on the door. "Cassie? Cassie, open up or I'm coming through."

He paused, counted to five, and when there wasn't a hint of sound or motion from inside, he stepped back two paces and turned his shoulder toward the door.

But before he could launch himself, the porch light snapped on, the neighboring door opened and a long shotgun barrel poked through. "Hold it right there," a man's voice said. "Drop the weapon and don't move. I'm calling the police."

Seth froze in his tracks and hissed a curse between his teeth. "I've already called them. I'm an FBI agent and I believe Officer Dumont is in trouble."

"Sorry, but I'm not letting you bust into Cassie's place without a look at your badge, mister." The door opened fully, revealing that the shotgun owner was young, probably early twenties and baby-faced with it. But he held his pump action with the ease of familiarity, and an infant's fretful cry emerged from inside, followed by a woman's soothing tones.

Seth could have the guy down in two seconds flat, but a new father with a gun? He didn't want to go there. So he said, "I'm going to go for my ID, real easy, okay? I don't want any trouble."

It took him under a minute to pull his ID and convince Cassie's neighbor he was legit, but those seconds beat beneath Seth's skin like the echo of a faltering heartbeat.

Finally, the guy lowered his shotgun. "Sorry. I just needed to be sure, what with Cassie being a cop and all." He rubbed his temples as though he had a headache, but focused his slightly bleary eyes on Seth. "What's wrong? Has something happened to her? Do you want me to go in with you?"

Untrained backup could be worse than no backup, so Seth shook his head. "No. Get inside with your family and lock up."

Then Seth took two running steps and slammed into the door. Pain sang through his body, but the heavy wood held. He cursed and tried again, wishing this crap was as easy as it looked on TV.

The door gave on his third try, splintering around a sturdy dead bolt. He kicked it the rest of the way in, convinced now that there was something wrong. There was no way Cassie could have missed hearing that racket.

He took a step inside her place. And smelled gas.

Her half of the house was full of it.

"Out! Get out!" Adrenaline sizzled through Seth's body. He raced back onto the porch and hammered on the neighbors' door. "There's a gas leak! Get your family out and warn the neighbors."

Then he ran back inside Cassie's home and swept the main room with his flashlight, barely noting the accents she'd added since his last visit, unexpectedly feminine touches of chintz and softness. "Cassie?"

No answer.

Knowing the gas leak was no accident, he

turned for the kitchen, hoping it would be that simple. No such luck. The stove and oven were both electric.

Damn it. The gas was coming from the basement. The bastard must have rigged a furnace line to fill her side but not the adjoining half of the house.

Seth took a guess and yanked open a door off the kitchen, hoping she had basement access. He was rewarded with a flight of stairs stretching downward beyond the flashlight beam. He eased down, moving fast but testing each step for a tripwire or pressure pad.

The smell was less intense in the cellar, suggesting that the gas line had been looped into one of the forced hot air vents.

When Seth reached the bottom, he shined his light over the dusty space, picking out a neat stack of cardboard boxes, a discarded bicycle, a hot water heater, and finally the furnace.

He froze and cursed at the sight of a wire-laden device duct taped to the tank. As he watched, the red numbers of the digital display ticked from twenty-one to twenty.

Then nineteen.

He spun and ran for the stairs. No time. There was no time to disarm the device, even if he had the knowledge. Once that thing blew, the spark would follow the gas trail up into the house. He had to get Cassie out of there, fast.

Seventeen. Sixteen.

He pounded up the stairs to the kitchen while the numbers counted down in his head. His flashlight beam carved through the darkness ahead of him as he bolted up to the second floor and shined the light into a short hallway, a bathroom, a bedroom.

No Cassie.

Fifteen. Fourteen. Thirteen.

Damn it. Where was she?

He reversed direction and charged down the stairs, heart pounding in time with the seconds left on the digital timer.

Twelve. Eleven. Ten.

He skidded back into the living room, aware that the slightest spark, the smallest flame, and it was all over. His head spun with the foul air. Desperation pounded in his veins, along with the sudden, all-consuming fear that this had been a setup, that she'd been taken, that both of them would be presumed dead in the blast and nobody would know to look for her.

Then he heard it.

The faint moan came from behind an overstuffed sofa. He staggered when he turned toward it, and a foggy piece of his brain told him that wasn't a good sign. "Ca-Cah-shee?" Hell, he was slurring like a drunk.

Got to get out of here, he thought as he circled the couch and shone his light down.

He saw Cassie lying motionless on the floor behind the sofa.

Five. Four.

He dragged her up. His muscles felt like putty and his coordination was off. He nearly fell, but forced himself to lift her, to stagger toward the door.

Got. To. Get. Out. Of. Here. The words hammered in his brain, strengthening his legs and arms. He could hear sirens in the far distance, agitated shouts closer by, but the inside of the house was deadly silent.

Three. Two.

He ran for the broken-open door, putting one foot in front of the other by sheer willpower as the seconds ticked down in his brain.

One. Zero.

Boom.

Chapter Four

Only the explosion didn't come.

Seth staggered out onto the porch and into blessed, clean air. He sucked in a huge lungful and pushed himself down the front stairs on rubber legs.

Cassie's neighbor broke free from the knot of people milling in the street and charged across the muddy lawn. "Let me help. Come on, we've got to hurry. The house could blow flat any minute."

"I can…walk," Cassie said, and struggled weakly.

Seth set her on her feet. "Don't walk. Run. There's a bomb in the basement."

But the countdown in his head was at minus five seconds.

The three of them bolted across the front lawn just as two BCCPD cruisers and the chief's four-by-four screeched to a halt nearby.

Seth pushed a dazed Cassie toward her neighbor and told the guy, "Make her sit down. As soon as the ambulance gets here, have the paramedics check her over."

He didn't like how disoriented she seemed. Maybe it was because she'd inhaled way more of the gas than he had. Or maybe there was something else. Had she been hit? Drugged? Anger surged through him. He'd find out soon enough, and then there'd be hell to pay.

She went with her neighbor rather than arguing, confirming that she felt terrible. If she'd had even an iota of her natural temper, she never would have let him order her around. That knowledge, that vulnerability tugged at him.

But instead of following and standing over her until the paramedics arrived, he forced himself to meet the chief halfway across the street, which was rapidly filling with neighbors. "Everyone's out of the house. Cassie's rooms are full of gas and she was inside, unconscious. I'm betting she was either knocked out or drugged." He took a deep breath of clean, cold air and felt his stomach pitch with the after-effects. "There's a detonator in the basement, but it didn't go off. Must've been a dud."

Even saying the word made his head spin. He'd been so sure of the explosion. So certain of death as those numbers had ticked down in his brain.

The chief barked orders as new sirens joined the melee. Sawyer and his bomb squad arrived on the heels of the ambulance, while the Bear Claw cops ushered the crowd back and cleared out the surrounding houses, just in case the structure blew.

Seth stood aside and looked over to where

the paramedics worked on Cassie. In the flashing lights of the rescue vehicles, her skin carried the waxy blue cast of a corpse.

If he had gone upstairs to his hotel room instead of turning back around, she would have died. The knowledge fisted in his chest with a pressure unlike anything he'd felt in a long, long time.

Knowing it, hating the emotion and fearing it at the same time, he gritted his teeth, turned away and stalked to where the chief was conferring with Sawyer at the back of the bomb squad van.

"We can't send in the remote because of the terrain," Sawyer said. Whip-thin and bald beneath his BCCPD baseball cap, the bomb squad captain was known for his quick mind and long, agile fingers. Now, those fingers tugged at the brim of the navy and yellow cap, and frustration narrowed his brown eyes. "The technology just isn't good enough to get the robot up a flight of stairs, through the house, through a door and down into the basement. It'll have to be one of my men."

They quickly discussed and discarded several other plans including fiber optics and sound wave technology. In the end, Sawyer went in himself, wearing a flak jacket, shield and respirator, which seemed like pitiful protection against the possible blast force.

A tense five minutes later, he radioed in. "There's a detonator, but Varitek's right. It's a dud. The readout is in the minus digits by ten-plus minutes, but it looks like the charge fizzled."

Ten minutes, Seth thought. He and Cassie should have died. He couldn't really get his mind around the concept, couldn't find anything inside except cold numbness. Then a spurt of anger.

It was true. The killer had targeted Cassie.

"I'm disconnecting it now," Sawyer's voice reported. There was a pause, then, "It's disarmed. If it was ever armed in the first place. This is a damn crude setup compared to the pieces we recovered from the canyon and the lab. You sure it's the same guy?"

"We're not sure of a damn thing," Chief Parry responded, but he kept his voice low enough that the nearby civilians couldn't hear. "What's the deal with the gas?"

There was a pause, then Sawyer said, "The line to her side of the two-family was patched over to the forced hot air ducts. Sloppy but effective."

And that very sloppiness was a problem, Seth thought. The explosive devices used against Alissa Wyatt during the kidnapping case had been sophisticated designs. Not sloppy. But what did that mean? Had Croft planted the earlier devices? Was this a different perpetrator, not a partner?

Seth scowled and grabbed the radio. "Don't disturb anything more than necessary. We'll need to get in there and process the scene."

The scene. He wasn't sure whether it helped or hurt to think of Cassie's home as a crime scene. On one level it helped distance him, helped remind him that this was the job. But on another level it rattled him to think of how close she had come to death.

How close they both had.

"What have we got?" Cassie's voice spoke at his shoulder, making him flinch.

He spun and scowled down at her, noting that her color was better but her eyes were still unfocused, her legs slightly wobbly. "Get back to the damn ambulance until they figure out what's wrong with you."

Her eyes focused and narrowed. "I know what's wrong with me. I was gassed. Before that, I was grabbed and injected with a tranq. And don't you dare tell me what to do. Not when there's a scene to process."

"Glad to see you're feeling better," Seth growled, "but there's no way in hell you're processing that scene. You're too close to it. And besides," he pushed on her shoulder hard enough to send her staggering back two steps, though he stayed close enough to catch her if she went down, "you can barely stand. I don't want you falling down and screwing up the evidence."

She drew breath to argue, then paused and let it out again. "You're right. I hate that you're right. You process it."

"I don't think either of us should be on scene right now," he said. His professional side itched to climb down into the basement and get a look at the device, at the furnace patch, at the living room, at all the things the bastard might have touched. But he wasn't willing to take the risk of screwing something up if he was shakier than he thought.

Besides, he wanted Cassie out of there, the sooner the better. It was tempting to figure they were safe surrounded by Bear Claw cops, but what if they weren't?

Their perp had broken pattern so many times already that he didn't have any damn pattern left.

"What do you suggest we do?" she challenged. He saw from the spiky anger in her eyes that she knew damn well what they should do. She just didn't like it.

"We need to call in the FBI's mobile unit."

She lifted her chin, but didn't argue, probably because Chief Parry was still standing opposite them.

"Good idea," the chief said as Sawyer emerged from the house, walking carefully. "Call them in." His eyes flicked to Cassie. "With Wyatt and Cooper away, you're out of backup."

But Seth didn't move. He spread his hands and waited until she looked full at him. "What do you say? This is your case. Your evidence. I'm just the muscle."

For now.

She held his gaze for a long moment, then her shoulders slumped with defeat, or maybe relief. "What the hell. Call your people. This isn't about my territory anymore, is it? It's about catching a killer before he catches me."

VARITEK DROVE HER to his hotel in silence, and pretended to browse through the brightly colored ski brochures racked near the door while she rented a room of her own.

"Will this be cash or charge?" asked the bored-looking desk clerk.

Cassie swallowed hard when she realized she didn't have either. She didn't even know where her purse was. It might have fallen in the first moments after she was attacked. It might have been stolen altogether, though the bastard clearly wasn't after money. A bubble of emotion lodged in her throat. Anger, maybe, or frustration. Not fear. She wouldn't accept fear.

She gritted her teeth and turned to where Varitek feigned interest in the spring skiing rates at Bear Claw Peak. "Can I borrow a credit card? I'll pay you back," she said quickly, more for her own benefit than that of the desk clerk or Varitek himself. "Better yet, I'll get the P.D. to pay you back."

Saying it that way steadied her and beat back the awkwardness. They hadn't yet talked about the fact that he'd saved her life. She didn't even know where to begin, or how to process the surge of joy she'd felt when she regained consciousness and found herself cradled in his arms.

"For the lady's room," Varitek's deep voice said at her elbow, startling her. She hadn't seen him move, but there he was, standing beside her, sliding a credit card across the counter.

The warmth from his body reached out to her, tempted her to lean. Her head ached, her arm hurt where the needle had left a fist-sized bruise, and she was tired. So tired. She had the almost overwhelming desire to ask for a hug.

Instead, she wandered over to the brochure rack while Varitek paid for her room, and tried not to feel as though it was somehow tawdry.

The impression was only magnified when they rode up in the elevator together and he followed her to her door. She didn't bother asking why. She already knew.

"I'll pass the clothes out in a minute," she said, tight-lipped.

He shifted, and she thought she saw discomfort in his cool expression. "Sorry, no can do. I've pushed it as far as I can by letting you leave the scene. I'm not willing to let the evidence out of my sight. If—and it's unlikely, but still—if we get something off your clothes and I wasn't in the room when you changed out, then there's no chain of evidence." He spread his hands and something like regret flickered in his eyes. "No chain of evidence, no evidence at all."

"Fine." She forced the word between her tense lips because he was right, damn it. She should have stripped on-scene. Who knew what contact evidence her attacker had left on her? Maybe nothing. Maybe something. But she hated that once again, Varitek had control of the situation, control over her.

She jabbed the keycard into the electronic door lock and pushed through. The room looked like any other midpriced hotel room she'd ever seen—beige and generic with the odd splash of color and polished wood. There was a bathroom to the right of the door with a closet beside it, and then the room opened up into a large rectangle with a big bed.

A really, really big bed.

The tawdry feeling increased a thousand-fold when Varitek followed her through. She wondered whether this was what a wife felt like when she started an affair, knowing it was wrong but not able to stop the momentum that had built up.

Not that she and Varitek were going to have an affair, of course. But stripping for him was pretty damn close, official business or not.

He made a noise that sounded halfway between a laugh and a growl, and crossed to the full-length sliding window at the far side of the room. He pushed the curtain aside and looked down at what she assumed was the parking lot. His shoulders were tense, as though he was looking for their perp out there among the four-wheel drive vehicles and their ski racks.

But when he spoke, his voice was low as a lover's. "They stock hotel robes in the closet."

She slid the mirrored door aside and found a heavy terrycloth robe folded and sealed in plastic. No doubt it would go on Varitek's credit card, too.

"Fine." She told herself that this was nothing, that they'd agreed to keep their relationship professional. "I'll leave the door open to preserve the chain of evidence. Okay?"

"Okay." His voice was gravelly and pulled at something deep inside her.

She swallowed hard and stepped inside the narrow bathroom, with its waist-high counter, double sink and soft piles of folded towels.

And began to strip.

HE HEARD A ZIPPER slide down, and the soft sound of shoes being kicked aside, and focused his attention on the parking lot, which was lit with orange sodium lights.

There was no sign of a watching presence, but one prickled along his nerve endings like a warning. A threat. He scanned the area again, looking for a misplaced shadow, a telltale hint of motion, a—

Cloth rasped against cloth, derailing him. No matter how hard he stared out the window, he was too aware of Cassie in the bathroom, taking off her clothes, piece by piece.

Leaving her naked.

"You got a paper bag for this stuff?" she asked suddenly, her voice as loud as if she'd been standing beside him.

A faint quiver in her tone betrayed...what? Nerves? Excitement?

No, he told himself with a mental curse. Call it what it was. Stress. For God's sake, in the space of two days she'd been involved in a foot pursuit, had her brakes sabotaged and nearly been killed in her own home. Now she was being forced to strip in front of—or behind— a near stranger. There was no way she found this titillating.

The fact that he did was, frankly, a little disturbing. But he was ultra-aware of her every motion within the small bathroom, hypersensitive to each rustle of cloth, each small noise. He pictured her removing her shirt, imagined her unfastening her jeans and sliding them down over the long, sleek lines of her legs.

He had to clear his throat before he said, "I didn't bring my kit up," which just went to show that he was off-stride. He never went anywhere official without the toolbox full of evidence collection basics. "There are paper bags for the dry cleaners in the closet. That should do."

A good evidence tech learned to improvise.

"Can you pass me one?"

"Sure." Seth forced himself to cross the room with a measured pace and reach inside the closet casually, as though this were a normal evidence collection.

As though he wasn't picturing Cassie naked, sitting on the marble counter between the double sinks, knees parted slightly in invitation.

"Get a grip," he muttered. He scrubbed a hand across his face and felt stubble rasp. It had been a long day, that was all. His anti-Cassie defenses were low.

"Varitek? The bag?" Her voice wrapped around the corner between the closet and the bath, making it all too clear that she was mere feet away.

"Here." He hooked his arm through the bathroom door and shoved the bag in her direction, then returned to his window. He pressed his palms against the cool glass and summoned up a memory of Robyn's face, not as he'd last seen her, bloodied and dying, but as he'd known her in life, sassy and snappy and always ready to stir up trouble.

In that, she and Cassie were alike, he realized, and was faintly disturbed to find himself comparing the two as he struggled to ignore another rasp of cloth from the bathroom. It wasn't going to happen between him and Cassie. He wouldn't *let* it happen. He wasn't ready for a new relationship, and was pretty sure he'd never be ready for someone like Cassie.

She was too much damn effort, like Robyn.

He and Robyn had worked on their marriage, sometimes harder than it seemed like they should have. When he looked at his sister's marriage, it seemed like CeeCee and Jack glided effortlessly through the years and the children. In contrast, he and Robyn had busted their butts to get along. They'd gone through three counselors and two sets of mediation sessions, but they had refused to give up, even when things were at their worst. Seth because he believed in one marriage for life. Robyn because she didn't mind fighting. Hell, sometimes she seemed to enjoy it.

And when you came down to it, they'd

stayed together because while they hadn't always liked each other, they had loved each other.

"All set," Cassie's voice said at his shoulder. He turned to find her standing there with one hand clutching a bulging dry cleaner's bag and the other holding her robe shut.

A faint blush stained her cheeks and he could see the pulse at her throat. It beat fast, as though she were nervous.

He took the bag. "I'll enter this into evidence and have someone from my team pick it up as soon as they get into town." When her eyes darkened, he sighed and said, "I know you don't like my people being involved, but what other option do we have? Call Fitz back?"

Something kicked at the back of Seth's brain when he mentioned Bear Claw's dinosaur of an ex-crime-scene analyst.

Cassie shook her head. "No. You did what you had to do. I don't like it, but I understand."

As though suddenly realizing that they were

standing dangerously close, she backed away, giving him a flash of her bare feet. Her narrow toes were tipped at the ends with a hint of pink polish that was completely at odds with the woman he knew as Cassie Dumont.

That fragile pink, that hint of vulnerability, only served to underscore the fact that she was wearing a hotel robe with nothing underneath.

Seth clamped his jaw. "I should go. Once my people get to your house, I'll have Marcy call you. She can sign some clothes out of the scene for you." In retrospect, he should have snuck a change out for her in the first place, but he'd wanted the scene processed by the book.

She dipped her chin in a nod. "Thanks." Then she pressed her lips together. "But don't think this means you're in charge of the case. I don't care what the chief says, or what you think. This is my case, not yours. Once your people are done processing my..." She faltered and swallowed, before continuing, "My house, they can turn around and head back to Denver, or wherever your field office is."

"You know damn well it's in Denver," Varitek snapped, annoyed. "And don't tell me what to do with my team. Have you stopped to think that we could use their help? That you're a one-woman shop in the middle of a case that's looking way more complicated than any of us thought?" He took a step closer to her, then realized it was a mistake when her feminine scent reached out to him, reminding him that she was wrapped in a single layer of terrycloth belted at her waist.

Instead of backing down, she narrowed her eyes to blue slits. "Oh, no you don't. Don't even dare. We had an agreement, remember? I'm in charge of this case, not you."

He growled, attraction giving way to rising irritation. "Be logical. Alissa and Maya are away for at least another week and you're a damned target. Do you really think the chief is going to let you out in the field if the bastard is looking for you?"

"The chief isn't going to *let* me do anything," she hissed. "He's going to expect me to do the job I was hired to do. Nothing more, nothing less. And if you get in the way of that, I'll…"

She left the threat hanging, but Seth didn't care to ask *you'll what*? He spun on his heel and headed for the door. It was either that or he was going to grab her and—hell, he didn't even know what he'd do. Shake her until her teeth rattled. Kiss her until the frustration either bubbled over or went away.

Neither was the right answer.

Once he had the door open and one foot in the hall, he turned back. "Get some sleep. We'll deal with this in the morning."

He tried not to notice the fine smudge of a bruise developing on her cheekbone, or the faint shadows beneath her eyes. She was no more fragile than the iron roses his metalworking sister crafted for fun—pretty and indestructible at the same time.

But even those roses could shatter if they were heated wrong. So he paused when he knew he should shut the door between them. "You going to be okay?"

A shadow flickered in her blue eyes, there and gone so quickly he didn't even know precisely what he'd seen. "I'll be…" *fine*, he could see her start to say, but then she stopped and corrected herself. "I need a weapon."

He nearly snorted at the incongruity of a beautiful bathrobe-wearing blonde with pink toenail polish demanding a gun.

Then he saw she was serious.

"You'll be safe here," he said. "You're on the fourth floor. I've got a room just down the hall. Nobody's going to get at you."

"You don't know that," she countered, voice low. "He got into my place. He got into the apartment building where the body was found. What's to say he won't get in here? Hell, it's a hotel. All he needs to do is rent a room." She held out a hand. "Your weapon, Varitek. I'm sure you've got a spare or two."

She didn't flinch when he glowered, didn't back down when he cursed. Finally, he reached down, yanked up his pant leg, and pulled out his spare piece. "Fine. Have it your way. Nothing new about that."

He slapped the smaller weapon in her palm, and this time got no sexual thrill from the contact. He was too stirred up, too irritated, though there was no good reason for the mood.

She closed her fingers over the gun. "Varitek, I—" Then she stalled, looking up at him. Faint color stained the base of her throat, where cloth gapped a little over skin.

"What?" he snapped as the heat rose between them like an unwelcome friend.

She looked away. "Nothing."

He nodded sharply. "Yeah. That's what I thought. I'll see you in the morning."

And he shut the door between them before he did something really, really stupid.

Chapter Five

Cassie was on the room phone before Varitek's footsteps faded in the hallway carpeting. To hell with the long distances charges—it was on his card, anyway. She knew the cell number by heart, and waited two rings, then four before the line went live and Alissa's breathless voice said, "Hello?"

A bass rumble sounded in the background, a low, intimate laugh that brought an uncomfortable twist to Cassie's midsection and revved her system back to the point where it had been when she'd stood too close to Varitek and forced herself not to reach out and touch.

"Hello?" Alissa's voice asked again.

Cassie forced herself to breathe. "Hey, Lissa. Am I interrupting something?"

When she heard another low murmur, she knew damn well she was interrupting and wished she hadn't called.

"Cassie!" Alissa's voice sharpened with concern. "Is everything okay? What's wrong? Are you hurt?"

"I'm fine," Cassie answered quickly, even though she wasn't really fine. Her arm stung where she'd been injected with God—and the biochemists currently testing her blood sample—only knew what, the back of her head hurt where she'd presumably banged it at some point, and she felt icky all over, like her attacker had touched her, only she wasn't sure where.

Finally allowing herself to feel the violation she'd held off while Varitek was in the room, she sniffed back tears.

"Cassie, talk to me." Her friend's voice grew stern and Tucker's background sounds quieted. Alissa continued, "You're not fine. I know what fine sounds like."

You won't be able to hack it in the field, Lee's voice jeered. *You'll come crawling back in a few weeks. You're not tough enough to cut it as a cop.*

Cassie's stomach twisted. She was being selfish. Alissa and Tucker were on their first joint vacation, celebrating the fact that they'd managed to live together for the past month without killing each other. She was tough enough to handle this on her own. "I'm fine, really," she said, voice stronger. "I just wanted to see how you guys are doing. It's quiet here."

There was silence on the line. Cassie could almost feel her friend trying to decide whether to buy it or not.

When Alissa spoke again, her voice was lighter, teasing. "What's the matter? No hot date? Stuck home alone on a Saturday night?"

God, was it really Saturday? Cassie thought furiously and realized that it was. She forced a laugh. "Come on, this is me you're talking to. My idea of a hot date on a Saturday night is pizza and *See Spot Run* with my next-door neighbors and their new baby." Which was a surprise. She hadn't figured herself for a baby person. But go figure, she'd taken one look at little Eden and melted.

That thought brought another, darker realization.

Eden could have died, along with her parents, Dean and Mary McGlaughlin, for no better reason than because they were her neighbors.

Anger sparked alongside the soreness of the day. When Alissa didn't say anything, Cassie went with a half-truth. "Okay, so maybe I'm a little lonely. It's silly, I know. The three of us have only been in town together for five or six months. I know how to entertain myself, it's just…" She trailed off, realizing her words were more than a convenient excuse.

"It's just that of the three of us, you're the one the other cops still aren't sure about,"

Alissa finished for her. "Are you ready to think about easing up on them yet? You know… you'll catch more flies—"

"Oh, please!" Cassie snorted, amused despite the situation. "If I wanted a lecture on making friends in Bear Claw, I would've phoned Maya." Which was one of the reasons she hadn't called Maya. "Never mind. Pretend I never called, okay? I was just having a moment."

Tucker's baritone rumble rose in the background and Alissa murmured something husky in response, setting off another low flare of envy in Cassie's stomach.

Alissa's voice returned, "Why don't you hit the chocolate I know you've got stashed behind the canned veggies? This sounds like something brownies might fix."

Except that her secret stash—a holdover from her days of living with her father and brothers—was blocked by crime-scene tape and she couldn't even go out for ice cream because one, she had no clothes, and two, she'd become a target.

Tears pressed alongside hysterical laughter. Cassie swallowed both and managed to say, "Yeah, that's a perfect idea. Thanks, Lissa. I'll let you and Tucker get back to…whatever you were doing. I'll see you next week."

She cut off the call before she broke down and asked her friend to come home.

Once the phone was back in its cradle, Cassie scrubbed both hands across her cheeks. "God, I'm a mess."

Her face felt oily and sticky, as though it were a stranger's skin being touched by a stranger's hands. Shivering, she checked the dead bolt on her door before heading into the bathroom. She laid Varitek's drop piece—a nifty little SIG-Sauer that fit her perfectly and probably looked ridiculous in his hand—on the vanity before stripping off the hotel-issue robe.

Then, before she could talk herself out of it,

she nipped back out into the hotel room, stark naked, and crouched down in front of the mini-fridge.

It was Saturday night, damn it. A drink wouldn't kill her.

She bypassed the hard stuff and grabbed two small cans of something that purported to be a premade mudslide. Figuring that was almost like eating a brownie, she opened one can and took a long swig.

The stuff was thick and chocolaty, and though calling it a mudslide might be optimistic, she felt a little warmer when the alcohol hit her stomach.

Part of her wondered whether she should be combining alcohol, natural gas and whatever sedative had been in that needle, but after the second sip, she decided she didn't care. She drained the first can, carried the second mudslide into the bathroom, popped the top and toasted herself in the mirror. If she'd ever deserved a drink, tonight was the night.

Besides, it wasn't like she was driving anywhere, she thought, and watched her haggard-looking reflection smile sourly. Her truck was impounded as evidence, and even if she had wheels, she had a feeling Varitek wouldn't let her go far. Knowing it, she drank the second mudslide and cranked on the shower full blast, set to parboil.

Damn, she felt nasty. She could swear she could feel her attacker's fingerprints all over her body. Her clothing had been properly tucked in when she came to, but still she hated that she'd been vulnerable to the bastard, hated that—

She shivered involuntarily and avoided completing the thought. She was fine. She'd gotten out in time.

Yeah, thanks to Varitek.

"Shut up!" she said aloud, because she didn't want to owe anyone anything, and certainly not him.

A little tipsy, more than a little grossed out

by the fingerprints she swore covered her breasts and thighs, she turned and climbed into the tub. Once she was under the blasting hot water of the shower, she sighed with pleasure.

The imaginary fingerprints washed away, along with the greasy feel of violation. She scrubbed herself from head to toe twice, then stood directly under the spray so it beat down on the back of her neck. Slowly, a coldness she hadn't even been aware of began to melt. Her stomach loosened and her shoulders dropped.

It was okay.

She was okay.

The words beat a litany in her head, and she realized that she was shaking. It wasn't until she sniffled and tasted salt that she realized she was crying, too. A sob bubbled up from somewhere deep inside her and erupted before she could choke it down. Another followed, then another, until her ribs locked up and she had to press her palms against the water-warmed tiles to keep herself upright.

Oh, God. I could've died. I almost did.

She remembered arguing with Varitek on her front porch. He'd wanted to look around, she'd wanted him to leave her alone. She'd opened her door, stepped inside and turned to close it. Then—

Nothing. She didn't remember a thing until she heard him shouting, felt his arms holding her, felt the waves of sickness inside her, all around her. Swamping her, consuming her.

Controlling her.

Chilled now, though the water was still scalding hot, she shut off the spray and leaned against the cool wall for a moment, waiting for the room to stop spinning.

"I'm a little drunk," she said, and was startled at how loud the words sounded in the echoing bathroom. She grabbed a towel from the rack, wrapped it around her torso and wobbled out into the main room.

She cursed when she saw that the message light wasn't blinking. Marcy—Varitek's only female forensics tech—hadn't called. "The jerk forgot to ask her about getting my clothes."

No doubt her predicament had been lost amidst more important details, like ordering up manpower to take over her case, her city. Her job. Who knew? Maybe calling in Varitek was the chief's way of saying he didn't want a dedicated forensics department. Maybe he was thinking of shutting them down and outsourcing.

What would Alissa and Maya say if they came home to pink slips? They would try to be brave about it, Cassie knew, because they were classier, kinder people than she. But the three friends would be split up again, sent to cop shops elsewhere in the state.

You need to try making friends, Alissa's voice said in Cassie's brain. Or maybe it was Maya's voice. God knew they'd both been on her to ease back, chill out, try to get along. But she hadn't bothered, because she'd been so damn sure she knew better.

Cassie's eyes threatened to fill again and she snuffled back the tears. She'd never been a weepy drunk before, and she didn't intend to start now. Besides, she could feel the glow wearing off by the moment, leaving achy tiredness and bruises behind.

Out of nowhere, determination grabbed her, driving away the shakes and the tears. She'd show them. She was good enough. Smart enough. She had the class ring they'd found, along with a few other bits of evidence from the grave. She had the hat and jacket from the guy who'd messed with her brakes. Let Varitek's people have her house.

She was going to solve the case from the other end.

Stone cold sober now, and almost sorry for it, she pulled on the hotel robe and tucked Varitek's backup gun inside, where the terry-cloth belt would hold it in place. No way she was going back to the lab unarmed. Hell, it was bad enough she was going there nearly naked. But she had a change of clothes in her office, and it was late enough that she could probably get herself through the back entrance without seeing anyone in person.

Yes, she'd show up on the security cams—the ones that had been suspiciously blanked when the lab was sabotaged during the kidnapping case. The other cops were sure to print off some ridiculous picture of her wandering the halls in a bathrobe and nothing else, but she told herself she didn't care.

They already didn't like her. It didn't matter if they hazed her further. What mattered was getting to the bottom of this case, identifying the murderer and protecting Bear Claw.

Her city.

Knowing this was the best answer, the only answer, she called down to the front desk and asked to have a cab meet her at the back stairs. When the phone rang to let her know the cab was in place, she gathered the robe around her with as much dignity as she could muster, took a faint breath of confidence from the body-warmed weapon cinched at her waist and headed out the door.

Varitek could go to hell. She had a case to solve.

IN HIS ROOM, Seth paced as he made the necessary phone calls, organizing his technicians and calling in favors, threats, whatever it took to get the job done yesterday.

His system was tight with too much energy and no outlet. He would have liked to go for a run, but he couldn't leave Cassie unprotected. She was safe a few doors down the hall, he told himself, and for the fifth time in a half hour, stopped himself from checking.

He already felt a sting of guilt that he was holding her hostage through lack of clothing. His team wouldn't be able to release her belongings until the following afternoon at the earliest. Until then, she'd be trapped in her room wearing a robe.

When Seth's mind locked on the image of long legs and fluffy white terrycloth, he wondered whether his plan was entirely ethical. He was doing this for her own good, he told himself, but the words rang hollow in his head.

Knowing he was a better man than that, he called down to the front desk. "Officer Dumont needs a change of clothes." He didn't elaborate, but kept his voice steely, daring the desk clerk to comment. "I can't leave her, so I need you to send someone to that 24/7 megamart down the street. She'll need everything from the skin out. Shoes, too." Seth thought a moment and tried to keep it impersonal when he said, "She's about five-ten, probably one-thirty. Skinny, but she's got muscles, and—" He broke off, realizing the clerk didn't need to know any of that. "Damn it, just get me some sweats and underthings. A few toiletries. Socks and a pair of sneakers that look like they'll fit a tall, slender woman. Got it? She needs something she can get out the door in."

Granted, he didn't intend to hand over the clothes until the next day. She was going to rest if it killed him.

The silence on the other end of the phone dragged on so long that Seth thought he'd been put on hold. But then the clerk's voice returned, sounding confused as hell. "Sir? You're referring to the lady in Room 421, correct?"

"Of course," Seth snapped. "The one I checked in on my card. Why? What's wrong?"

"She asked me to call her a cab an hour ago. She's gone."

"Damn it!" Seth slammed down the phone without another word. "Stubborn—" He stopped himself before he said something he'd regret. But he didn't stop the forward motion. He yanked on his boots and laced them with quick, angry jerks.

A stream of curses worked its way between his teeth. She just hadn't been able to wait for him. She just couldn't force herself to trust that maybe this time he was right, maybe this time she should stay put and let everyone else do their damn jobs.

As he jammed his weapon into its holster and drew faint comfort from the fact that he'd given her his drop piece, Seth realized he was muttering to himself.

"That's fine," he said aloud. "She's going to get more than a grumble when I catch up with her." He grabbed his jacket and dragged it on over the holster. "In fact, she's going to wish she'd never left."

And if as he stormed out the door and down the stairs to the parking lot, a little piece of him realized he was overreacting, he decided it didn't matter. She'd knowingly endangered herself—again—and had disobeyed a direct order. Again. It almost seemed like she was *trying* to get herself killed.

If so, he'd be damned if she did it on his watch.

CASSIE HAD EXPECTED the lab to feel a shade creepy. Hell, it hadn't felt totally safe since the blast that had destroyed all of their equipment and had nearly killed Alissa.

The bomber shouldn't have been able to get inside the P.D., shouldn't have gotten in and out undetected, but he had. For a time, there had been whispered suspicions. *What if he's a cop? What if he has access?* That would've explained a number of seeming coincidences, like how the bastard had known which car was Alissa's and how he'd slipped an anonymous envelope into the P.D. under the desk sergeant's nose.

When Bradford Croft confessed, the missing girls were found and there was no evidence of another person's involvement, the whispers had died down. It wasn't a cop, after all. The perp was just lucky.

Or very smart.

Now, Cassie wondered as she laid out the bagged pieces of evidence on a wide, waist-high table in the main lab. The overhead light was harsh and unnatural, underscoring the windowless walls. But where fatigue had dragged at her back at the hotel, now a fine quiver of nerves and focus sharpened her senses and drove her brain at top speed.

Could there be a cop involved? Could that be why they were making so little progress on the new murder, why the older case had hit so many roadblocks along the way?

Her gut twisted at the thought, but her brain picked through possibilities. If anyone was going to see it, she would, because she wasn't one of them. She was an outsider, whether she liked it or not.

While her brain tweaked at possibilities, she picked up a shallow plastic container filled with a muddy liquid. When she moved the jar, metal clinked on plastic as the class ring swirled at the bottom. She'd dipped the ring in a mild astringent solution earlier, before the task force meeting. She and Varitek had agreed there would be little hope of pulling trace evidence off the ring, which had been buried too deep for too long, amidst the freeze-thaw mayhem of the Colorado frost line. So their best hope was that the ring would prove to be an identifier.

Since they didn't have the skull anymore, they would have to work the ancillary evidence.

Humming tunelessly beneath her breath, Cassie selected a pair of blunt, rubber-tipped tweezers and used them to lift the ring from the jar. She'd examine the sediment later, if the ring proved unhelpful.

"But you're going to help us, aren't you?" she asked, telling herself it was okay to talk to the evidence, because there was nobody else in the P.D. basement to hear.

A skeleton crew of cops manned the desks and phones above her. Task force members buzzed in and out, though there had been little progress on IDing the dead man. There was movement overhead, giving Cassie a faint sense of security.

Added reassurance was provided by the

motion detectors Chief Parry had ordered installed after the lab bombing. The alarms could be armed or disarmed a room at a time, so Cassie had reset the motions in the rooms between her and the stairwell. She was wearing her spare clothes and had a gun, there were cops on the floor above, and two rooms worth of alarms between her and the outside world.

So why didn't she feel safe? Why was she so aware of the open door at her back and the darkness outside?

"Stop being a weenie," she said aloud, and focused on the ring. On the evidence. On the case.

Her case.

The astringent had eased away the grime and gunk, leaving the brassy metal as clean as new. A quick visual scan showed that the ring was worn thin at the bottom, which surprised Cassie. The ME had tagged the skeleton as belonging to a young woman, late teens, maybe early twenties. That wasn't much time to wear a class ring to thinness, suggesting one of two things. Either the ring was a hand-me-down from a friend or relative…

Or it didn't belong to the body at all.

"It was buried a layer down," she reminded herself, and had a brief thought of turning on the radio for background noise. But her mind quickly skimmed ahead of the inconsequential details and focused on the thought process that marked her as a good evidence tech. Maybe not a brilliant one, but a good one. A thorough one.

It was true that the ring hadn't been precisely *in* the gravesite. It could've been lost years ago, or it could've been dropped by a passing hiker and wound up mixed in with the grave fill.

"Work the evidence, not the hypothesis," Cassie reminded herself. It wasn't about whether she wanted the ring to belong to the girl or not, it was about what she could empirically determine about the evidence.

Knowing it, she carried the object across the lab to the stereomicroscope. She set the ring on the platform and pressed her eyes to the scope, preferring the old-fashioned immediacy of the eyepieces over the distance of sending the image to computer.

The ring looked like gold plate over a duller, silver metal. She could see where the gold had rubbed away and the silver—stainless steel, maybe?—shone through. There were scuffs and scratches on the outside of the worn section, as though the wearer was used to physical labor.

The decorated upper part of the ring had a flame insignia opposite some sort of animal. The metalwork was crude enough that she couldn't tell whether it was a bear, a boar or a dog. The carvings flanked a red stone, probably a ruby, though not a high quality one. She saw the cloudy streak of a flaw within the stone, and a fine crack along one edge.

There was no date, which was a shame, but

when she flipped the ring over, she could just make out the worn shadow of a maker's stamp. Three letters that looked like PRK or maybe PEK.

It wasn't an easy answer, but it would do for a start.

Cassie typed shorthand notes on a small computerized notepad while she scanned the ring, knowing it was best to record even the smallest observation right away. Sometimes, first impressions were the most telling.

That thought brought a flash of memory, a hint of the first time she'd seen Varitek. The chief had sent her to the airport to pick up the FBI interloper, and she'd been justifiably ticked off over the whole thing. Tangled with annoyance had been her concern for Alissa and the kidnapped girls, and a slash of shame that she was small enough to care about her turf when there were victims to worry about.

She'd used her badge to pass through to the gate area. When she'd seen a tall, broad-shouldered man duck through the door as though he was used to banging his head, her first thought had been *wow*. Her second thought had been, *Oh, hell. That's got to be Varitek*. His dark, commanding presence matched the voice she'd already heard on the phone, as it had barked commands and tossed off demands as though she should be happy for the help.

And perhaps she should've been, but she wasn't, and she was even less pleased to learn that the owner of that deep, dark voice wasn't five-foot-six, as she had secretly hoped. At five-ten, she topped a good many men, much to their annoyance, but she doubted too many people had ever topped Varitek. Worse, she doubted he even cared, an impression that had been reinforced as he'd hefted his field kit and walked in her direction, as though he'd made her for a cop without a second's hesitation.

"Officer Dumont," he'd said in greeting, and she'd been insulted by how fast his eyes had skimmed over her and passed on, as though she had been registered and dismissed that quickly.

"Varitek," she'd acknowledged, consciously leaving off his Special Agent status as though she didn't give a hoot. "Let's get one thing straight. I didn't invite you and I don't want you here. The Bear Claw crime lab can handle this just fine without the FBI sticking its nose into the case."

His eyes, a pale green surrounded by incongruously long dark lashes, had returned to her, this time locking on as though he was actually seeing her. He'd raised one dark eyebrow to an inquisitive line, but said, "If you could handle the case, your chief wouldn't have asked for my help."

The conversation had gone downhill from there, Cassie remembered, and was surprised to find herself a little wistful for that first moment of meeting him, before things had gotten complicated by attraction and history and work. For an instant as he'd stood framed in the airport doorway, she'd seen him as a man rather than an obstacle. And in that moment, she'd like what she was seeing. Then she'd gotten to know him a little, and that liking had been quickly lost to irritation. Aggravation. Dislike.

You like him just fine, that little voice said, *aggravation and all*.

"Oh, shut up," she said aloud, and forced herself to snap out of it and get on with the work.

She keyed in her final few notes, and then lifted the class ring in the rubberized tweezers before she pushed away from the stereoscope and scooted her rolling chair back to the main table. Once there, she reached down beneath the table to grab a plastic evidence baggie, thinking to reseal the evidence before she turned to a computer check of class ring distributors and designs.

As she straightened, she caught a swing of motion in her peripheral vision and her heart jolted. *She wasn't alone anymore!*

She didn't waste time wondering who was there or how they'd gotten past the motion detectors in the outer room. She lunged out of the chair and grabbed for the SIG-Sauer she'd tucked into her waistband at the small of her back.

"Oh, no you don't," a deep voice growled. Strong hands grabbed her wrists and powerful arms pinned her body. She screamed as she was spun around and pressed against the basement wall, right beside the security system hub, which glowed green across the board, indicating that it had been disarmed.

The breath hissed from her lungs as the weight of her attacker's body pressed her into the wall. Her heart hammered against her chest when she looked up into familiar light green eyes that told her two things.

One, her attacker was Varitek.

And two, he was furious.

Chapter Six

The feel of Cassie's lithe body against his did nothing to calm the rage that thundered through Seth. He grabbed the front of her wrinkled shirt and twined his fingers into the material, holding her in place so there could be no avoiding it when he growled, "What part of *stay in your room* don't you get?"

He didn't bother to ask if she was okay. She seemed fine, save for a few bruises from earlier in the day—yesterday now, he supposed, since it was nearing dawn.

Her eyes narrowed and she hissed, "You're not my keeper. You might outrank me, but we're in different agencies so I'm not even sure it counts. And you sure as hell don't get to order me off my own case. The chief told me to work the skeleton." She struggled against him for a moment, then stopped when he didn't budge. She bared her teeth. "I was following orders, *Special Agent* Varitek. Just not yours. Which is the problem, isn't it?"

"I'll tell you what my problem is, you—" Seth bit off the words.

His problem was the images that had slammed into his brain the moment he'd realized she was gone. His problem was hearing an "officer down" call on the radio as he'd driven like fury to get back to the P.D. He should have been relieved when the call had turned out to be two uniforms dealing with a convenience store holdup, but the images hadn't stopped. They caromed through his mind in a twisted blend of memory and prescience, vivid pictures of Robyn's blood-smeared face and Cassie's limp form sprawled behind her living room couch.

The farther he'd driven, the less he'd seen of Robyn and the more he'd thought of Cassie in trouble. Cassie being chased, grabbed, beaten, tied up, blown up, a hundred deaths that he'd seen on the job, echoes of a thousand crime scenes, a thousand victims' families crying over their losses.

He twisted his fist in her shirt. "It's not about giving orders, it's about being stupid, Cassie. What if he'd seen you leave the hotel?" He jerked his chin at the green-lit security board. "That's a bad joke. I had it disarmed in under a minute."

He didn't bother to mention that the unit's designer was a former Bureau man who'd shown him the trick. He wanted her good and scared.

But instead she came right back at him, hissing, "And I would've had you flat on your back thirty seconds after you touched me if I hadn't recognized you."

He snorted. "Baloney. I've got weight, height and reach on you. You couldn't take me if your life depended on it. In fact, I bet you—"

She snaked a foot behind his ankle, planted her opposite knee in his solar plexus and knocked him to the floor. His breath whooshed out of his lungs more from surprise than impact, and he lay there for a moment, sprawled half-beneath the wide lab table.

Cassie flowed to her feet with more skill than he'd expected from an evidence tech, and pressed the sole of her canvas sneaker across his throat. "You don't grow up with four brothers without learning that quicker beats bigger every time."

Before Seth's rational side could protest, he grabbed her foot and twisted sharply to bring her down. He threw out an arm and caught her waist to break her fall, then when she grabbed his arm and parried with an elbow jab to his throat, he decided enough was enough. He pinned her squirming body to the floor with his full weight.

Aware that he was likely crushing her, he scowled down. "Quicker's better than bigger, eh? Now what are you going to do?"

Her face was flushed and she breathed heavily beneath him, but she didn't look the slightest bit cowed. "I'm going to fight dirty. Just remember, you asked for it."

He expected a knee to the crotch, and tangled his legs around hers to guard against the move. But he was unprepared for her to reach a hand between them and grab his tender flesh as though she were going to squeeze and twist.

Shock and a roar of heat paralyzed him for the half second she needed, and she neatly reversed their positions so she straddled him, literally holding him at her mercy. But instead of flashing with triumph, her eyes darkened. Instead of crowing with victory, she hitched in a breath and a dark flush washed up her neck, visible in the bright fluorescent lights.

Seth knew damn well what she was feeling. He might try to tell himself that this was about the job, the case, her protection, but it was really about the two of them, about the fact that he couldn't be in a room with her and not feel the heat of attraction that had bound them together since the first moment they'd met, when he'd been polite and she'd bitten his head off.

It wasn't love at first sight. There would be no second chance at love for him. But it had been *want* at first sight. Lust at first sight.

At least on his part.

And looking up at her, at the way the pulse pounded at her throat and her tongue moistened her lips as he watched, he had a pretty good idea the feeling was mutual.

"Ah, hell," he said, and reached up for her the moment she leaned down for him.

Their lips met halfway as though that had been the plan all along.

ONE MOMENT she was kicking his ass and the next they were lip locked. Cassie wasn't quite sure how it had happened, but in the first moment of contact, when she tasted his breath and felt the faint rasp of unshaven stubble, she knew it was the only way this could have ended.

During their wrestling match, she'd flashed back on an early lesson from her middle brother, Rick—the one entitled "What to do if your date doesn't get the word *no*." She'd grabbed Varitek, not thinking of the consequences.

But in that first moment, when she'd become profoundly, intimately aware of his excitement, part of her admitted that she'd known precisely what she was doing. Precisely what she wanted to have happen.

This, she thought as she opened her mouth to him. She invited his tongue, demanded it and twined the fingers of her free hand into his shirt to keep herself from taking the kiss further, taking it all the way as her body demanded.

This was what she'd wanted, what she needed. This was the flash and the flame she'd been missing with the men she'd dated since Lee. This was the power and the demand.

And, she realized as he rolled them so they were on their sides, hip to hip, meeting as equals, this was what she'd feared, because how could she not give up control to a feeling as big as this one?

The heat roared through her alongside need, alongside the desire to chuck rationality, to chuck her carefully constructed defenses and give in to the pleasure of flesh against flesh, strength against strength. Almost without her permission, the fingers of her free hand strayed from his shirt to his close-cropped hair and the heavy muscles of his upper arms. It wasn't until he groaned and swept a hand down her back to her hip and urged her closer that she realized her other hand still cupped him intimately.

He reached down and urged her hand boldly up another inch, until she was touching the heavy, hard length of him though his jeans, which were soft with wear and time. He groaned and pressed himself into her hand as though he was helpless to do otherwise. He loosened her shirt from the waistband of her pants and touched the skin of her belly, her ribs, reminding her that her spare set of clothes hadn't included a bra.

Or underwear.

Knowing this was foolish, stupid, all the things she'd told herself before but that didn't seem so important now, she murmured and kissed him, letting her tongue and touch encourage him, incite him.

Needing no more urging, he cupped one of her breasts in his palm and dragged his thumb across her aching nipple, setting free a shower of sparks within her system. She bowed back on a wash of pleasure, and when he shifted to rise above her, she freed both hands to pop the snap of his jeans. The top of his member rose free from his briefs, and she teased her thumb across it, collecting a single drop of fluid, a pearl of want that spread across his skin, loosing the smell of sex. Of desire.

Too fast, a voice chanted in the back of her head. *Too fast, bad idea!* But she ignored it because it had been too long since she'd felt this way—hell, had she ever felt this way? She didn't think so, knew only that her body was crying for release, for completion.

For Varitek.

Hell, for Seth. She should probably practice using his first name at this point.

Refusing to let reality intrude, she kissed him again, and gloried in his skilled touch at her breasts her belly, her sides, the pulse at her throat. It seemed his hands were everywhere, inciting, inflaming.

Need pulsed within her alongside the knowledge that they were separated by only a few layers of clothing, that it would only take—

Footsteps sounded on the basement steps.

Fear sluiced through Cassie, a cold dose of the reality she'd been trying to avoid. She froze.

Holy hell. She was making out with a coworker on the floor of the crime lab.

The footsteps drew closer—several sets of them—and a man's voice said, "The desk officer said she was down here. The security system's off, but I don't see anyone."

The sounds passed into the outer office area as Cassie and Varitek jerked away from each other.

Caught, Cassie thought. They were so caught.

And then they *were* caught. Tucker stepped into the doorway with Alissa flanking him on one side and Maya on the other. Alissa's honey-colored hair was pulled back in a workable ponytail and threaded through a BCCPD ball cap, and her pale eyes were wide with shock. Maya was darker and more formally dressed, and hid her surprise beneath her counselor's veneer, while Tucker's habitual untamed air was lost to amusement.

Cassie yanked her hand out of Varitek's jeans and hoped to hell the others couldn't see that his arm disappeared at the elbow beneath her shirt. "Hey, guys. I was…we were…"

She faltered, too aware of her friends' shock and the fact that Varitek had barely reacted at all. He stared fixedly over her shoulder, jaw clenched as though he was furious. At her. At himself. She wasn't sure, but his response tightened something sick and unsettled in her gut.

"I can see you were," Alissa said, voice strangled. "And here I was thinking you were in trouble after you phoned. I called Maya and we decided to come home. You sounded so strange, like there was something going on." Her eyebrow rose. "I can see there is. When did Special Agent Varitek get into town? That *is* Varitek, right?"

That brought him off the ground with something between a curse and a roar. He reached down and hauled Cassie up as though it was no effort whatsoever—leading her to wonder whether she'd won their wrestling match after all, or whether he'd let her win. She glanced down and was grateful to realize that her shirt was more or less retucked and his fly was fastened, though she wasn't sure when he'd managed either.

Varitek shoved his hands in his pockets as though that would camouflage his physical state. "Yeah, it's me. And regardless of what you just saw, we've got a serious problem. The Canyon kidnapper's partner has surfaced. He's graduated to murder, and he's targeted Cassie."

"Cass?" Alissa took a step forward as Tucker moved to guard her back. "Are you okay?"

"I'm—" *fine* she started to say, but Varitek interrupted.

"Her brakes were tampered with and her house was nearly flattened last night with her in it. She won't be fine again until we find this guy. Hell, nobody in Bear Claw will be safe until we do." He pushed away from her and stalked past the others. Once he was through the door, he turned back and glowered at her. "Stay here with your friends. Tucker, you're with me."

Then he was gone, his retreat marked only by angry bootfalls on the stairway.

Tucker glanced at Alissa. "I'll deal with him and see what the chief has to say. You three watch each other's backs, okay?" And then he was gone.

After Tucker's footsteps faded upstairs, Cassie was left facing her two best friends, who looked like they couldn't decide whether to razz her about getting caught making out with Varitek or yell at her for not telling them that the task force had been reinstated.

Suddenly overwhelmed by the events of the past few days—danger, the stress, the lack of sleep and the heat that had soured so quickly in the face of Varitek's anger—Cassie leaned against a wall, put her face in her hands and began to laugh like a banshee.

It was either that or cry.

But when she felt her friends' hands on her shoulders, one on each side, she pulled it together, knowing she was better than this. Stronger than this.

She sniffed. "Okay, guys. Let's get to work. We have a class ring to identify." Then maybe she could catch a few hours of sleep on one of the cots they'd stashed in the back room. She was suddenly exhausted.

But the case had to come first. They had a murderer to catch before he struck again.

IN THE DEEP DARKNESS before dawn, when Bear Claw City slept, the hunter took to the streets again. He was utterly, arrogantly sure that his prey would be alone this time. He knew because he'd been the one to stand her up. It was Saturday night. Date night. He had offered to get her into the Natural History Museum—still closed for renovations—and give her a sneak peek at the new exhibit.

She'd seemed more interested in the privacy than the artifacts. Slut.

Well, she would get her date now—on his schedule, not hers.

He eased his vehicle to the curb outside her house, parked and left the engine running. The main house was empty this time. She'd told him her father had gone back east for the weekend on business and her mother had tagged along for a change of scenery.

She'd winked as she said it.

The roads and walkways were dry this time, the mounds of dirty snow nearly gone. Still, he watched for the melting piles as he followed the stone pathway around to her door, wanting to leave no footprint, no clue.

The Bear Claw cops would have to work with the evidence he chose to leave them.

She had locked the door this time, but left it unbolted, as though inviting him in with one hand but using the other to punish him for making her wait.

He smiled in anticipation. He knew about punishment. About waiting. Soon, she would, too.

He dealt with the lock and eased the door open with no more caution than he'd used before. He was that confident in her.

Sure enough, she lay perfectly still in her narrow bed. The heat was up in the basement room, making the air steamy and too warm. She had solved the issue by kicking the covers away to reveal stocking-clad legs beneath a high-slit skirt. His keen dark vision showed him that her white shirt was rucked up past her lacy bra, revealing a smoothly toned young stomach defiled with a belly button ring.

Anger stirred in his gut at the sight of her, at the wanton sprawl of arms and legs and the faint snore that escaped from between her painted lips.

He stepped closer, hands clenched into fists. An empty glass on the bed stand suggested that she was not so much asleep as passed out. She'd drowned her sorrows when he didn't come for her on time. Bitch. Slut. Whore.

The anger rose within him, pure and perfect

and cleansing, and he reached for her, wanting to—

Stick with the plan, the voice whispered inside his head, or maybe from behind him, through the open door that was letting the heat out into the yard.

Yes, right. The plan. The hunter forced himself to take a deep breath and go through the steps in his mind. He wouldn't be sloppy. Sloppiness had killed Croft.

Sloppiness and the cops, that is. But he was smarter than the cops. Hadn't he already proven that? He was better than the police in this city.

You're not better than anyone! a deep voice bellowed in his head, making him cringe even though he knew the memories couldn't hurt him. They were just that. Memories. The owner of the voice was gone.

And buried.

He relaxed his fingers and forced himself to breathe in and out, in and out, until his heartbeat leveled and he was back in control. This was no place for temper and passion. Not here, not now.

That would come later, once he had her where she belonged.

Proud of his control, he stepped toward the bed and eased his arms beneath her, until she was cradled against his chest by her neck and knees. The power flowed through his body when he lifted her, making the dead weight seem like nothing.

She murmured softly and curled into him, her breath smelling of alcohol, her muscles lax and compliant.

"I've got you," he murmured against her temple as he carried her from the room and shut the door behind, to keep in the heat. "Everything will be perfect now, don't worry. I've got you."

AFTER SETH LEFT Cassie and her friends down in the crime lab, he appropriated an upstairs conference room and spent the wee hours of the morning riding his team to process the scene at Cassie's house as quickly as possible. When his techs stopped answering the phone, he focused on searching the databanks for comparable murders. Similar patterns. Anything.

Through it all, he wished like hell he'd never come back to Bear Claw.

"You want to talk about it?" Tucker asked from the doorway just as dawn stained the sky outside.

Seth grimaced. "Nothing to talk about, really. We'll have Cassie's place processed in another hour or so—they're not finding much of anything—and we'll be back to spinning our wheels over the boy's murder."

Tucker dropped into a nearby chair. "That wasn't what I meant."

Seth stared at his laptop screen for a moment, as though focusing on it would force the databank to cough up a pattern, a matching murder. Then he sighed and slapped the laptop computer shut. "I know. I just—" He cursed and scrubbed a hand across his face. Felt the rasp of stubble and made a mental note to shave before the task force meeting. "Why? You doing the stand-in big brother thing on Alissa's orders?"

Not that Seth would blame him. That had been a hell of a scene they'd walked in on. Even now, several hours and some serious reflection later, the memory of those hot, steamy kisses was enough to make him hard and wanting and all twisted up inside.

But Tucker snorted. "Cassie's got plenty of brothers. She wouldn't thank me for trying to be another one." The lean, rangy homicide detective leaned back in his chair. "I'm asking as a friend, and because Alissa was nearly killed before. If we didn't get the bastard, or if there's another one out there, she could be in danger again. I need to know that you're not...distracted."

Seth scowled. "Don't talk to me about professional detachment. When Alissa was abducted, you threatened to tear me limb from limb if I didn't help find her."

An almost feral glitter darkened the detective's eyes. "Exactly. He came after my woman. Now he's coming after one of her friends. One of *my* friends. And I want to know that your head is in the case." He held up a hand to forestall Seth's angry retort. "I'm not saying it's fair. Hell, I'm tempted to ship Alissa back to the island until this is over, just in case the bastard decides to go after her again. But I won't. Do you know why?"

"Because she'd kick your ass for suggesting it?"

One corner of Tucker's mouth twitched. "That, too. But also because she's a cop. The chief might look the other way over some fraternization within the ranks, but he expects us to do our jobs. He expects us to act like cops."

Seth knew that. He knew it down to his very core. But knowing it and liking it were two different things. Cassie wasn't just a cop, she was a cop with something to prove, which was a damned dangerous combination.

Seth shoved back from the table and locked eyes with the homicide detective. "I can't promise to be impartial—hell, I don't know what I am at the moment—but I swear I'll do everything in my power to help the Bear Claw P.D. get this guy. Deal?"

Tucker regarded him for a long moment, then nodded. "Deal." Then he grinned, though the expression was tense at the edges. "And speaking of professional detachment and the lack thereof…I asked Alissa to marry me last night."

"HE ASKED YOU to *what*?" Cassie nearly screamed. The noise bounced off the basement walls and reverberated among the pieces of equipment. "Ohmigod. Tell me what he said. What you said. Everything!"

Cassie and Maya crowded close while Alissa

held out her left hand, newly christened with a big, fat diamond in a platinum setting.

"I was…" Alissa touched her throat with her hand, causing the ring to flash and sparkle under the fluorescent lights. "Shocked doesn't even begin to describe it. When the three of us moved here, the first thing I learned was that McDermott was on his way out of the force, that he never stayed still for more than a couple of years, that he was the footloose kind. And now this…" She trailed off and a soft smile touched her lips. "I knew it was right between us. I was even ready to move with him if he wanted to keep wandering. But he says he's home. He wants us to stay here for good, maybe even buy a bigger place." The grin widened into a full-blown smile. "We could live in a tent for all I care. I'm that happy."

And for Alissa, with her unsettled childhood and deep desire to put down roots, to say something like that…

It was real.

Cassie hugged her friend, overjoyed. But deep inside, she felt a twist of something nasty, something she wasn't proud of and didn't like. It wasn't jealously, precisely, it was more like a wistful question.

Why not me?

It was only recently, after Cassie first started hanging out with the neighbor's baby, that she'd realized she wanted a family. Which— at least in her opinion—required a husband and a house. Future plans and 401Ks. All things she hadn't thought about in a long, long time, ever since Lee had dangled those promises with one hand, and tried to snatch away her career with the other.

Several years of hindsight and a brief stint in therapy allowed her to acknowledge that she'd given him that power, bit by bit. She'd been blinded to his true nature by the passion that had flared between them. She had stupidly equated good sex with a good relationship.

How wrong she'd been.

Which brought her thoughts full circle to Varitek. She'd kissed him in her own lab. Hell, she'd done more than kiss him. She'd groped him, encouraged him, tangled herself around him until they'd been moments away from—

Well, something stupid, that was for sure. What had she been thinking?

Clearly, she hadn't been thinking at all.

She drew back from her three-way embrace, and gave Alissa's ringed hand a final squeeze. "I'm so happy for you two. I mean it. You're perfect together."

Alissa snorted. "No, we're not. We disagree with each other, push each other, challenge each other and…" She sighed. "Yeah, we're perfect together." Then, before Cassie could process that definition of *perfect*, Alissa poked her in the arm. "So what's going on with you and Varitek?"

"There's," *nothing going on,* Cassie started to say, but didn't bother because all the evidence pointed to the contrary. "It's compli-cated, and it was a mistake. One I'm not planning on repeating. Let's just leave it at that and get back to the case."

Anyone else might have respected her wishes and moved on, but the three friends knew each other too well. Maya tilted her head to one side and asked quietly, "Are you okay?"

"No, I'm not okay," Cassie snapped on a quick wash of resentment. "My truck was im-pounded, my house is a crime scene, my arm hurts where I got a needleful of the black market sedative-of-the-week, my head aches where I banged it, and I cabbed here in a damn *bathrobe*." Aware that her voice had risen on the last word, she took a breath and fought for calm because none of it was Maya's fault. "The thing you saw with Varitek, it was just stress. Temporary insanity. There might be some attraction between us, but that's all it is."

"And how do you feel about that?" Maya asked in her counselor's voice.

Cassie sighed, confused. "He could shut us down. You've heard the rumors—that it'd be cheaper for the chief to call in outside help when he needs it rather than keeping us on staff."

"Rumors are just that," Alissa said quickly. "We're an asset to this department and the chief knows it."

"If you say so." Cassie didn't believe it for a minute. "But if that's true then how come the FBI has been all over our two major cases so far?"

Because you're the weak link, Lee's voice whispered in her head. *If you could hold up your end of the job, Varitek wouldn't even be here.*

"Because they're major cases," Maya said. "Most local shops bring in FBI oversight for multiple kidnappings or murder."

"Oversight." Cassie's lips twisted. "Yeah, that's me. An oversight." Then she straightened. "But not anymore. I think it's time we go to war." She looked from Alissa to Maya and saw that the determination in their eyes mirrored her own. "Let's prove that the chief didn't make a mistake hiring us. Let's get this guy before he has a chance to kill again."

"Too late." Varitek's voice broke in from the doorway.

Cassie didn't know how long he'd been standing there, didn't know how much he'd heard.

She glanced over and didn't see any memory of their kiss in his eyes. He could have been carved from granite. He looked that cold when he gestured to the stairs. "Come on. There's been another murder. A woman this time." He took a breath and something passed across his face, an expression so fleeting she had hardly registered it before it was gone. But she caught an echo of it in his voice when he said, "Brace yourself. This one's bad."

Chapter Seven

As far as Cassie was concerned, no death was good, save perhaps for a dignified exit through old age or illness, one that gave enough warning for the family to gather and say goodbye but didn't linger much beyond. The other kinds were almost universally bad.

Her mother's death from a quick-growing form of breast cancer had been bad, especially for the family she'd left behind—four teenage boys and a five-year-old girl, alone with a grieving husband who'd done his best, yet hadn't always managed the details.

But murder was a different sort of bad.

"We're here," Varitek said unnecessarily as he

pulled in amongst a cluster of official vehicles at another anonymous apartment building.

He avoided her eyes as he unbuckled his seat belt and slid out of the truck cab. They hadn't talked about what had happened between them, which in a way made it seem worse, more important, until those kisses had become an elephant riding in the truck between them.

Hell, she didn't even know what she wanted to say. Maybe it was better to just let it go.

She jumped out of the cab and stumbled when she hit the ground. Her head spun and her stomach lurched unsteadily, but she braced her legs, refusing to let the weakness show. Maybe it was the bang on the head, maybe the drug, or maybe just plain old fatigue. Regardless, she wasn't giving up another crime scene.

Varitek paused on the sidewalk outside an apartment complex that was little more than a brown, characterless rectangle. "Come on. They're waiting for us."

They walked in together and she paused at the entrance, noting that the "locked" foyer door lock was banded with several duct tape layers of varying ages, allowing easy access for the renters.

Or a killer.

Still not speaking to each other, as though they'd had a fight she didn't remember, she and Varitek rode the elevator up to the fifth floor. When they stepped out into the drab hallway, the smell of death reached down Cassie's throat and grabbed her lungs, sucking the air out of them and sending a slap of panic into her bloodstream. She braced her shoulders and forced her footsteps not to falter, too aware of the big man at her back.

But when they paused outside the cordoned-off door, pulled protective equipment out of their kits and suited up, she realized that, oddly, the silence had become almost companionable, as though they'd been partnered for years and already knew each other's moves and thoughts.

Before she could enter the room, he held out a gloved hand to stop her. "Wait. We need to talk."

A spurt of alarm jolted through Cassie and she scanned the hallway, knowing that while she could trust Tucker, Alissa and Maya not to spread rumors, the other Bear Claw cops wouldn't be so kind. But the immediate area had been cleared of unnecessary personnel until the evidence technicians gave the okay.

Seeing that, she took a deep breath and squared off to face him on rubbery legs. "Fine. Talk."

He shifted to shove his hands in his pockets, realized they were gloved and let them hang at his sides. "Earlier, when I left the basement. I don't want you to think that I—"

"Don't worry about it," she interrupted, not wanting to hear the excuse. "In fact, let me make this easy on you. What we did down in the lab was fun, but it was a mistake. I'm not what you're looking for anymore than you're my ideal man. Let's just say it was the stress of the moment and move on, okay?"

She expected him to be relieved. Instead, he looked annoyed. "How do you know what I'm looking for?"

"I'm only guessing that you're looking for peace. Someone who won't pick fights. That isn't me. Besides—" she shrugged, gaining momentum now, feeling as though she was trying to convince both of them "—I know for a fact that you're not what I'm looking for. For one, I don't date cops."

He shifted close to her. Dangerously close. "I'm FBI."

"That's worse." Her head spun, forcing her to lean back against the nearest wall. "I grew up with four brothers watching my every move. I'm not looking for someone else to babysit me."

"What *are* you looking for?" He threw the question down like a challenge. A gauntlet.

A husband, she thought. Children. But those

wishes were too new for her, so she said, "Respect. I'm looking for a man who'll treat me as an equal rather than thinking he can order me around." Anger stirred in her chest, as memories of Lee and Varitek got a little mixed together.

Varitek scowled. "I don't—" Then stopped himself and his expression shifted to something she couldn't quite read. "Never mind. You're right. I don't know why I even brought it up." He gestured to the door. "Come on. We've got work to do."

He pushed open the door and gestured her through, not giving her time to brace herself. Refusing to show the weakness, she marched into the room and faced the scene of the crime.

She saw the body immediately. There was no way not to.

And yeah. It was bad.

The naked girl was propped up in an open sofa bed, with her arms stretched out along the back and a thin blood trail leaking from her severed index finger. The stump looked cauterized, similar to the murdered young man's finger. That particular detail hadn't been released to the media, which argued against a copycat.

Only this time, the killer hadn't stopped with the finger. The girl had been carved with a circular cut that removed her navel and laid her abdominal cavity open for their inspection.

Cassie swallowed her gorge, averted her eyes from the gaping wound, and tried to see the girl as she might have been in life. She'd been thin, blond and pretty, with long legs and good skin that was glossed with a touch of makeup. Her fingernails were expensively manicured, her hair cut in the latest style. Her sightless eyes were blue. Ligature marks at her neck indicated the same cause of death.

A cold, nauseous chill shivered through Cassie's stomach.

Looking at the victim was almost like looking at her own senior picture from high school.

When Varitek cursed low, she knew he saw it, too.

Pulse pounding, Cassie swallowed the nasty aluminum foil taste that had gathered at the back of her throat and tried to push past the awful reality of the girl's grayish blue skin to see the evidence beneath. She cleared her throat. "Same souvenir, same pose, except for…" She gestured at the girl's belly, where blood had leaked down to stain the sheet that lay across her spread legs.

Varitek nodded, his attention fixed on the body. "Yeah. It's the same, and she fits the pattern of the others—young, pretty, female. So what was the deal with the John Doe? And what's with the additional cut?"

"That's what we need to figure out."

Neither of them mentioned the obvious—that the girl could have been Cassie's sister.

Thinking that, Cassie realized there was a hell of a lot that she and Varitek didn't say to each other. She wasn't sure why, but the thought brought a surge of sadness as she set down her evidence kit, popped the top and prepared for the first round of photographs. The sooner they worked the scene, the sooner they could start putting the pieces together. The sooner they figured out what the hell was going on, the sooner they could nab this bastard.

Then Varitek could return to Denver where he belonged.

THEY PROCESSED THE SCENE for nearly three hours. By the time they were done, the new day had brightened outside the dingy studio apartment and Seth's knees were aching like fury, reminding him that he'd been going for nearly twenty-four hours and needed to catch some downtime before he dropped.

Cassie couldn't have been any better off— though maybe her tranquilized snooze behind the sofa counted as a nap—but he couldn't see the fatigue in her as she worked the scene, skirting the dead girl as wide as possible when she thought he wasn't looking.

"Time to call it quits," he said finally. "There's nothing else here." At least nothing he could see, and he didn't think that was fatigue talking. "Let's let the ME have the body. Maybe we'll get something off the autopsy."

She nodded and started packing the labeled plastic and paper evidence bags into her kit, but she didn't look any happier than he felt. "It doesn't make any sense," she said finally. "There should be more."

"Yeah. This guy's either very lucky or very good. Since we've got three other scenes that seem equally clean..." He trailed off, bothered by the fact that his team had found almost nothing at Cassie's house or in her truck, and they'd already come up nearly dry at the first murder scene.

Cassie nodded. "I know. I'm betting he's very good. Nobody gets this lucky four times in a row." She finished packing and stood, evidence kit dangling from her fingers. A shadow crossed her face. "We never did figure out how the bomber got in and out of the forensics lab without being seen. The security videos were all screwy, and nobody on the main floor saw anything before or after the fire drill that emptied the building." She cleared her throat and planted her feet firmly as though she'd only just noticed she was nearly swaying. "Add that to the lack of evidence, and I've been thinking that maybe…" She trailed off.

"Maybe it's a cop," he finished for her. "Yeah. I've been thinking along the same lines. I hate it, but it'd explain a few things that just don't work any other way." He jammed his hands in his pockets, shoulders tensing at the thought of the flak they were going to cause by bringing it up. "When we get back to the P.D., let's start by running the prints we've collected against the in-house database. We've mostly got partials, but if we keep the search parameters pretty wide, we might get something."

He hated the thought of doing the search

almost as much as he hated the suspicion that they were going to get a hit. He respected the Bear Claw cops. He didn't want it to be one of them.

But hell, he'd learned a long time ago that sometimes wanting something just wasn't enough.

IT WASN'T UNTIL Cassie sat down in the task force briefing room that she realized she'd just about kill for a bottle of water. A soda. Anything. Her throat was parched and the back of her tongue still tasted like tinfoil.

"Ugh," she muttered, and earned herself a startled look from Maya. As they had from the very beginning of their time in Bear Claw, the three women sat in a front corner of the briefing room, slightly separated from the rest of the group. Only now, instead of the three sitting shoulder to shoulder, Cassie and Maya sat together and Alissa sat one row back, beside Tucker.

Her fiancé.

Normally, Cassie didn't give a damn about the seating arrangements, but now they bothered her, reminding her that things had changed, that Alissa had moved on.

"And you need to get over yourself," Cassie said, only afterward realizing she'd spoken aloud.

"Cass, what's wrong with you?" Maya said, poking her. "You're squirming and talking to yourself. Can I get you something? A bathroom pass? Glass of water? Prozac?"

Cassie scowled at her friend's lame attempt at humor. "I'm fine. A bit of a headache, that's all. You got any aspirin? Maybe some juice? My system's whacked out from the lack of sleep."

"I'll be right back. Aspirin and juice coming up."

It wasn't until she'd gone that Cassie realized Maya was acting strangely. Or rather she was acting normally, but her voice was brittle and unfamiliar stress lines cut grooves on either side of her mouth.

Captain Parry started the meeting before the psych specialist returned. He took his position at the front of the room just as he'd done months ago, when they'd been racing the clock trying to find three kidnapped girls before they became a trio of murder victims. Then, the case board had been hung with school pictures of the missing girls.

Now, it bore photos of the dead. The crime-scene pictures—the first set shot by Cassie, the second by Alissa—were tacked behind Parry's head, alongside morgue shots that served as grim reminders of their goal.

What if it's a cop? The refrain beat in Cassie's head, in her heart, because she knew it made too much sense, fit too many of the small, contradictory details.

"Here you go." Maya returned and handed Cassie a couple of tablets and a bottle of vending machine fruit punch. "Take these, you'll feel better."

Of the three friends, Maya was the nurturer. Quiet, dark-haired and dark-eyed, she mothered them but asked for little in return, as though she had a limitless supply of patience and compassion. But as Cassie downed the juice and painkillers, she thought she saw cracks in Maya's normal calm strength.

As the chief brought the rest of the task force up-to-date on evidence Cassie already knew by heart, she leaned toward Maya and whispered. "What's wrong? You seem stressed."

Maya's shoulders slumped. "It shows?"

"Did something happen at the conference? I'm sorry you had to come home early. It wasn't—"

"Not the conference," Maya interrupted. "It's a case."

Cassie glanced around to make certain that their whispered conversation wasn't bothering anyone before she asked, "The murders? Do you have a theory?"

If the psych specialist had also started to suspect a cop then that was doubly good reason to get right on those fingerprints. Cassie glanced to the back of the room, to where Varitek habitually leaned against the wall, observing.

He was gone.

"Not this case," Maya answered, pulling Cassie's attention back to her friend. The other woman's fingers twisted against each other in an uncharacteristic display of nerves. "I'm having trouble with—"

"*As I was saying,*" Chief Parry raised his voice and glared at the women. "We've ID'd the first victim as Peter Dunbar, a ski instructor at Bear Claw Peak."

Chastised, Cassie sat back in her chair and focused on the briefing. But as the chief spoke, she made a mental note to grab Maya after the briefing. Something was going on with her.

Something bad.

"Peter Dunbar had no apparent connection to the apartment he was found in. The super claims the room's been vacant for nearly a month. The lease is still active, but the last known tenant—this Nevada fellow—took off weeks ago. The killer either knew the room was empty, or he got lucky."

The chief called Tucker up next. The homicide detective cleared his throat and looked grave. "A missing persons report was filed first thing this morning by parents who'd been out of town. Their nineteen-year-old daughter wasn't home when they arrived." He paused. "They positively ID'd the female victim as their daughter, Jasmine Gardner."

Oh, hell. Cassie's shoulders slumped. True, it was a break in the case. The names would allow them to follow up with Jasmine and Peter's friends, to see if they were connected to each other either directly or through a third party. But at the same time, assigning names and families to the dead was one of the hardest aspects of cases like this.

When Tucker retook his seat, the chief looked around the room, clearly searching for Varitek. With the FBI agent AWOL, Parry was forced to call on Cassie. "Can you update us on the forensics findings, Officer Dumont?"

She stood and crossed the room, thinking that she needed food or sleep or both, because she was feeling seriously funky.

She gripped the sides of the podium, which provided her a sturdy, solid anchor. "Reexcavation of the canyon crime scene yielded a class ring that appeared to have been associated with the skeleton." Was the room spinning or was it just her? "Early this morning, we were able to use the insignias and manufacturer's stamp to track the ring to Tyngsboro High School, outside of Boulder. Even better, we were also able to pinpoint a graduating year for the wearer. Our comparison of the class list to missing persons files has presumptively identified the skeleton as belonging to eighteen-year-old Marcia Pennington, who disappeared from her Tyngsboro home eight years ago this March."

Cassie's heart dragged at giving a name to yet another dead body, but she also felt the burn of satisfaction, of a job well done. Eight years after their daughter's disappearance, the Penningtons would finally know where she'd gone. They'd finally be able to bury her and say goodbye because of work done by the Bear Claw forensics department. It had been her work, not Varitek's, that had identified the victim.

But he wasn't even in the room to hear the announcement.

Where was he, anyway?

"Congratulations—you've ID'd an eight-year-old skeleton," a male voice called from the crowd, "but what about the current murders? They've got to be the priority right now."

There was a murmur of agreement, or maybe

that was the buzzing in her ears. Irritation spiked through the dizziness. "You want progress?" Cassie snapped, knowing she'd agreed to keep it under wraps but suddenly not really caring. The spinning sensation overrode caution, telling her it was time to stir things up. Time to give her coworkers a taste of their own medicine. Suspicion. Distrust. She leaned close to the microphone. "I'll give you progress. Hell, I'll even give you a suspect! Take a good look at each other, because—"

The microphone cut out with a squeal. Cassie spun in time to see Varitek advancing on her with a sheaf of papers in one hand, the microphone power cord in the other. "Outside. Now."

His words were clipped and his eyes snapped with temper.

She backpedaled a step, tripped on the power cord and nearly went down. Varitek dropped his end of the cord, caught her by the elbow, righted her and hustled her toward the door without breaking stride.

"Let go!" she hissed, aware of the other cops watching with expressions ranging from derision to avid curiosity. "Varitek, what the hell are you doing?"

He got her through the door and slammed it, cutting them off from the rest of the Bear Claw cops. "I'm saving you from blowing our chances to make a clean grab. What were you thinking?" He held up the papers. "I've got a match on one of the prints, and you were just about to tip off our only suspect. What's wrong with you?"   She focused on the name for a split second before realizing she had a more immediate problem. The juice roiled sickly in her stomach and the floor beneath her feet swayed like the deck of her brother Rick's fishing boat.

Oh, hell. She was going to be sick.

She broke away from Varitek and bolted for the ladies' room. She made it into a stall, barely, and was miserably ill. Even once her stomach was spent, dry heaves wracked her shivering body, doubling her over and making her long for oblivion.

Heavy footsteps sounded behind her. A large, warm presence crouched down beside her.

The last thing she remembered was the gentle touch of Varitek's hand.

The oblivion was laced with a single name.

Fitzroy O'Malley.

Their cop suspect.

Chapter Eight

Cassie woke up alone, in the dark, in a strange room. Panic flared quickly, then leveled when her blurry eyes focused in the dim light and she saw quiet, unlit monitors pushed back against the wall. She lifted her arms and saw no wires, no needles.

She was in a hospital room, but she didn't feel hurt, and it was pretty clear nobody was all that worried about her.

The latter thought pricked at her and she lay still for a moment, waiting for her memories to assemble themselves into something like coherence.

When they did, she almost wished they hadn't.

She groaned aloud. "You've got to be kidding me!"

She hadn't actually slammed two mudslides and taken a cab to work in her bathrobe, had she?

Yes, she decided, she had. Then she'd worked evidence, groped Varitek, and made a fool of herself in front of the task force.

Oh, hell. She braced for an insidious whisper, for Lee's voice to tell her she wasn't good enough, wasn't tough enough, that she should be happy with the junior instructors position he was sure he could get her.

But there was only silence in her head, in her heart.

Before she could question the why of it, the door opened and a shadowy figure slipped inside. Cassie's heart jolted and adrenaline flooded her body in a hot, hard rush.

"Oh, good," a soft voice said, "you're awake."

Maya! Cassie identified the voice and relaxed on a mild stab of something she didn't want to analyze too closely.

"You needn't look so disappointed." Maya turned on the bedside lamp, but kept it turned low, so the cone of white light illuminated the two of them but not the room. "He's been in and out all day. The chief ordered him back to the hotel for some sleep."

"I wasn't looking for Varitek," Cassie said quickly, but they both knew it was a lie. She sat up slowly, then when her head didn't spin and the nausea didn't return, she swung her legs over the side of the bed. A breeze blew straight up her backside, so she pulled the thin blanket over her shoulders. "What time is it? Strike that, what *day* is it? And what the hell was wrong with me?"

Maya sank into a chair beside the bed and leaned her head back against the wall with a tired sigh. "It's early Monday morning. You pretty much skipped Sunday entirely, thanks to what turned out to be a delayed reaction to the tranq."

"And a couple of drinks, some aspirin and a

fruit punch," Cassie muttered, finally remembering how damn sick she'd felt before she collapsed. "God, I was a mess. Why the hell did I think I was coherent enough to be at the P.D.? I should've been locked in my room."

"Varitek said he tried," Maya said dryly. "Something about stealing your clothes. Apparently, it didn't work."

"Unfortunately, no." Cassie scrubbed both hands across her face and was somewhat cheered to realize that although she ached all over, she felt sharp and ready to go. "Can I leave, or do I need a checkup or something?"

"The doc cleared you hours ago, but you were dead to the world, so we decided to let you sleep it off. We can leave when you're ready."

"The sooner the better," Cassie said quickly. "Varitek showed me some important evidence before I got sick."

"The fingerprints." Maya nodded, eyes somber. "He mentioned it to Alissa and me, but that's about it. I can't believe Fitz could be involved." She shook her head. "Are you guys sure about this, Cass? Fitz O'Malley may have reputation of being as good as he knew how. Doesn't it seem odd to you that he'd go bad at this point in his career?"

Cassie pulled the blanket around herself and dropped off the edge of the bed to stand on her thankfully non-wobbly legs. She strode toward a pair of closet-type doors, figuring one must have her clothes behind it. "Look at the evidence, Maya. We've had at least four incidents where the P.D. has been the focus of the criminal activity. This guy seems to slip in and out of the building without anybody noticing or caring. He knows how to tweak the cameras. That says cop to me."

"Perhaps." Though Maya didn't sound convinced. "But wouldn't people notice if Fitz suddenly appeared at the P.D.? He's supposed to be in Florida."

"The evidence doesn't lie," Cassie said. "The simplest explanation is usually the correct one. You said it yourself during the kidnappings. There were an awful lot of coincidences that made more sense when we looked at the P.D."

"I said 'someone with criminalist training,'" Maya corrected, sharply enough that Cassie turned back to look at her.

Unlike Cassie, Maya was never sharp, never cranky, never said things she didn't mean. Then again, she was also always perfectly groomed and put together, with her dark hair in a businesslike twist and her power suit tweaked into place.

But not right then, Cassie realized as she pulled her own clothes out of the shallow closet.

Maya's hair was twisted up, yes, but not with its usual perfection, and she was wearing pants and a sweater, with flat shoes. She was still put together, but not ruthlessly so.

And there were stress lines on her face.

Suddenly remembering their conversation

in the conference room, Cassie pulled on the fresh jeans and shirt that someone—probably Maya, as a matter of fact—had thoughtfully brought her. "You going to tell me what's up with you?"

Maya shifted uncomfortably. "I thought you were in a hurry to get back to the lab and look at those fingerprints?"

"They'll keep for a few minutes." Cassie was itching to get back on the job, but friendship had to come first sometimes. "Talk." She let the silence hang, a little interrogation trick she'd learned from Maya herself.

Finally, Maya sighed and let her head tip back against the wall. "I've been working with child services on a case, a little boy named Kiernan Henkes." She paused. "It's bothering me. Kiernan was hospitalized three weeks ago when he went to the school nurse with breathing problems, and she saw a mess of bruises on his ribs. Turned out he'd cracked one. He swears he fell out of a tree. His mother swears he fell out of a tree. His father told me to get the hell out of his face."

"Sounds like a charmer," Cassie said.

"You have no idea." Maya glanced at her. "Does the name Henkes ring a bell?"

"Should it?"

"The father, Wexton, is a fixture in Bear Claw politics. Old money philanthropist. He's funded most of the new exhibit at the Natural History Museum."

"Right." Cassie nodded. "Wexton Henkes. Anasazi artifacts. Got it. But if the kid says he fell out of a tree, there's not much you can do, unless there's a pattern of these 'accidents.'"

"No pattern." Maya twined her fingers together in her lap. "That was the first time he'd been in the hospital for anything beyond vaccinations and the occasional bout of strep throat. But…" She trailed off.

"But what?"

Maya pushed to her feet and paced the room

with uncharacteristic agitation. "I didn't like Henkes. He gave me a really bad vibe."

"You think he hurt Kiernan?" Cassie asked. She pursed her lips in a soundless whistle. "And you think I'm brave for going after Fitz O'Malley. Do you realize what you're talking about? That's playing politics, Maya. Could be dangerous, especially if you don't have any evidence."

"You think I don't know that?" Maya spun back, nearly shouting the words. "Do you honestly think I don't know how it works?" Then she froze, wide-eyed, and lifted trembling fingertips to her lips.

"Maya?" Cassie took a step forward, but the other woman backed away.

"No. It's okay. I'm okay. I'm just tired." Maya forced a laugh that sounded brittle and false. "I was here most of the night. I think I'll head home. Get some rest. Something."

She turned for the door, but Cassie said, "Wait. Stop. Talk to me."

Maya's face twisted and then smoothed as though the painful emotion had never existed. She said, "Don't worry about me, Cass. I'm fine."

Her expression was utterly calm as she said the words, with the soft serenity Cassie had grown used to. But now Cassie wondered whether it was an act, whether Maya was hiding something beneath that calm.

How had she missed this for so long? What sort of a friend was she?

Cassie turned for the shallow closet and grabbed her sneakers. "Why don't we go get a cup of coffee? I think we could both use one."

"Thanks, but I'm going to get out of here," Maya said. "I'll talk to you later."

She pushed through the door out into the hallway without another word. Cassie cursed and hopped on one foot, trying to pull on her shoes and chase her friend at the same time.

How had she not known about this? Because,

she realized, Maya rarely talked about herself, and never about the past. Everything with her was carpe diem. Seize the day. Live for the moment rather than looking backward or forward. It wasn't until that moment that Cassie realized that she didn't know a damn thing about Maya, unless it had happened at or after the police academy. The knowledge made her feel small, like she'd been so caught up in her own stuff that she'd taken her friend for granted.

"Hell," she said aloud, and took a step toward the door, intending to track Maya down and… well, she didn't know what she was going to say, but she knew the friendship was precious, knew that somehow she needed to help.

But a shadowy form darkened the doorway, filled the frosted window and paused outside as though uncertain of welcome.

Cassie's gut identified the figure before her brain had quite caught up with the rush of heat and the sudden acceleration of her pulse. *Varitek.*

Instead of waiting for him to knock and

enter, she yanked the door open and faced him squarely. "I don't have time to deal with you right now. I need to talk to Maya."

He didn't budge, just stood there and stared down at her, face expressionless, pale green eyes reflecting something she couldn't even begin to identify. After a moment, the corner of his mouth kicked up. "I see you're feeling better."

"Sorry," she said pausing when she saw that he had her jacket draped over his shoulder. "I don't mean to be rude. You caught me at a bad time."

"It happens." But he didn't step back when she moved to push past him. Instead, he held up two commercial airline folders. "Not so fast. We have a plane to catch."

Cassie looked at him in surprise. She saw the marks of strain and too little sleep on his face, and felt a spurt of guilt that he'd been working the case while she napped. "Where are we going?"

"Florida. The chief wants us to interview Fitz in person."

THE HUNTER FOLLOWED his new prey to her home, then the hotel where the FBI agent was staying. They spent under fifteen minutes at each location, emerging with small bags—one for him, one for her. Once they were on the road again, headed out of downtown Bear Claw, he followed at a discreet distance, confident that neither of them would pick up the tail.

His old man had taught him that the chase was part of the hunt.

He remembered following his father deep into the forest, trying hard to step in the big, widely spaced bootprints. Then the big man had halted and held up a hand. *Stop,* the gesture had said, then *Look!*

His boyhood self had frozen in place, an excited rictus of muscles that longed to twitch and run and play. Slowly, ever so slowly, he had turned, and—

A strident digital ring interrupted the memory, yanking him back to the highway and the surrounding cars. When the ring came again, he slapped at the dashboard button, annoyed. "Hello?"

"We have a problem."

The hunter was surprised to hear the voice emerge from the hidden speakers. There were days he was nearly convinced that the voice, and the plan, existed only within his skull.

"Did you hear what I said?" the planner demanded.

The hunter's equilibrium was off, with the past and present tangling around each other, along with the memory of a gunshot. A scream. Blood.

He swallowed. "Yes, I heard. I'm following the prey right now. The blonde and the FBI agent. They're headed out of town on the highway."

"They're going to the airport," the planner said. "To Florida. It's time to mix things up…I want you to follow them and take care of them down in Key Lobo."

The hunter scowled. "That's outside my territory." Like most predators, he had marked a space as his own. He allowed no other hunting in his territory, but by the same token wouldn't kill outside of it.

"Territories can be adjusted as necessary." The planner's voice chilled. "Do you understand?"

The hunter preferred to study his prey, to plan and predict the chase before he made his move. He disliked stalking outside of his comfort zone, disliked acting on impulse.

His father's advice rang in his head. *Plan the hunt, son. Plan the kill.*

Then again, sometimes the impulsive shot netted the greatest reward.

"Well?" the planner demanded. "Are you in?"

"I don't like it. It's not my style."

"I know, but with Bradford gone it's just the two of us, son. I need to know I can depend on you."

The word *son* laced itself around the hunter's

soul, touching a deep, dark place within. "Yes," he finally said, "you can count on me."

"Good." The planner's voice softened. "Do as I ask, son, and everything will be forgiven."

Chapter Nine

Varitek—she still couldn't think of him as Seth, never mind saying it aloud—slept through the nonstop flight to Southern Florida, but Cassie was too wired to doze.

She'd bought a paperback at the airport gift shop, thinking to entertain herself by dissecting the policework in the story. But once the big jet lifted off the runway, she was too jittery to read, too aware of Varitek's nearness and the way his shoulder and arm pressed against her. He'd used frequent flier miles to upgrade them to first class because the regular seats were too small for him, but he still crept into her space, warm and solid.

She watched him in spite of herself.

He didn't soften in sleep. He didn't snore, or

even relax all the way. He could have been carved in stone, all uncompromising angles and lines that made her think.

That made her wish for the impossible.

Thanks to the time zone change and a brief delay, they landed near dinnertime. Once the wheels touched the tarmac, Cassie turned to wake Varitek, only to find his eyes open and clear, with no residual sleep fuzz.

Either he was one of those people who woke up immediately, or he'd been faking it.

They spoke about small, inconsequential things as they deplaned and headed down to the rental car pickup. But Cassie was aware of the brush of their arms as they jostled together in the line and the touch of his breath at the back of her neck when he looked over her shoulder.

"Get something big. A truck or an SUV. I hate little cars."

"Already done." She edged away from him, unnerved by a flicker of sexual heat. This wasn't a romantic getaway. Hell, they weren't even romantic.

But still, she was hyperaware of him as they collected their rented SUV. She was attuned to his every motion as they stowed their gear and pulled out a map. The chief had wanted the questioning handled in a very casual fashion. He didn't even want them to go through the local P.D., which worried Cassie.

Varitek paused before climbing into the SUV. "Something wrong?"

She tried not to notice how his pale green eyes fixed on her with full attention, and how the intangible contact set up a warm jangle in her stomach. Damning herself for the weakness, she said, "I don't like this. We have a fingerprint match, so why not have the locals haul Fitz in for questioning? It feels like the chief is trying to spare his old friend's feelings at the expense of the case."

"I wouldn't let the chief dictate my investigation," Varitek said shortly. "We're here because we need to be." He jerked his head at the vehicle. "Get in and I'll explain."

Cassie bristled at his peremptory tone, but snapped a salute. "Aye, aye, sir."

Once they were on the road headed to Key Lobo, Cassie prompted, "So? Explain."

Varitek glanced at her, then returned his attention to the road, which was fringed with palm trees and grass visible under the street lights. "My people found three of Fitz's fingerprints—two partials at the first murder scene, one at the second."

"And?" Cassie demanded, tone sharp with annoyance at the involvement of "his people" when she should have been the one to run the analyses.

"They're all fragments of his left thumbprint."

"Oh, hell." Cassie sank back in her seat. While a thumb was a common enough print to find, the law of averages said that finding an index finger print was just as likely. "You think it's a plant?"

"Could be." Varitek hit the blinker and took the exit ramp leading toward the keys. "It's possible our perp got hold of a single print from Fitz and made a mold. I've got the lab testing for latex residues and synthetic oils now."

"But why bother framing Fitz?" Cassie asked, then thought a moment and answered her own question. "To throw it back on the police department. It always seems to come back to the Bear Claw P.D., doesn't it? Croft went after Alissa. The new guy went after me. The lab was torched." She paused while the passing scenery changed from neon tourist glitz to pastel residential areas. "He's after the police department." Then she contradicted herself. "Then why the elaborate kidnappings? The murders? Why not just target the P.D. directly?"

"Because this guy goes for the grand gesture," Varitek said. "You don't need Dr. Cooper to tell you that."

Which reminded Cassie. She needed to call Maya again. Her last two attempts had gone directly to voice mail, and Alissa reported that she hadn't seen the psych specialist all day.

Something was up.

Varitek continued, "What worries me is the fact that we might be playing into exactly what he wants us to do." He glanced at her. "Think about it. Why pick on Fitz? Why not one of the active officers?"

A shiver worked its way down Cassie's neck. "O'Malley retired awfully quick. What if he actually *is* involved?"

"And what if the killer wants us down here for some reason?" Varitek countered. "It's all a bunch of 'what-ifs' at the moment, at least until we figure out the story on the fingerprints and interview Fitz directly." He turned off the main road. "I think we should assume the worst until the evidence suggests otherwise. We're going to stick together and watch each other's backs. Okay?"

Cassie tilted her head to one side. "Watch each other's backs. As in partners?"

A muscle beside his jaw ticked. "For the time being. You willing to give it a try?"

For a crazy moment, she thought he was asking her something else entirely. Maybe it was the balmy, warm air caressing her winter-dried skin, or the night-shrouded greenery, which reminded her that they were far away from Bear Claw and prying eyes.

Maybe it was the strange intimacy of having sat beside him through the long plane ride. Or maybe it was realizing that even now, stone cold sober and awake, she wanted to reach out and touch him like she had down in the lab, when they'd been mindless for each other and had no thought for the consequences.

Then she looked up and saw that they'd pulled into a small motel. "Where the hell are we?"

He parked the SUV outside a neat, green-painted door marked "Office," unhooked his seat belt and dropped down from the vehicle. Before she could react, he opened her door and stood in the gap, not quite blocking her from exiting, but not giving her much room, either.

His eyes were intent as though he, too, knew they were having two separate conversations. "We need to wait on the results from the additional fingerprint analysis. It isn't worth talking to Fitz until we know whether or not the prints are legit." He glanced over his shoulder at the motel, which was modest but neat, a single-story row of numbered doors that gleamed with fresh paint in the glow of stained-glass-shaded porch lights. "It's late. I think we should get a couple of rooms, maybe go out for a bite to eat. I don't know about you, but I'm starving."

"I could eat," Cassie said carefully, confused by the sudden change in him. She tilted her head. "Why are you asking me rather than telling me?"

He stepped away and his features darkened ever so slightly. He shoved his hands in his pockets, rocked back on his heels, then said, "I did some thinking while you were sleeping off your ketophen-and-mudslide backlash. Maybe I've been out of line. You're a cop and an evidence technician, and you're good at your job. I haven't given you enough credit for that."

Cassie opened her mouth, but nothing came out. It took her a moment to recover. Then she said, "Wow. You come up with that on your own?"

His expression shaded toward rueful. "Not exactly. I took Alissa to your house so I could check on my team and she could grab your clothes. She, ah, pointed out that the way I treat you and the way I treat my female techs are light years apart." He looked away, but didn't retreat. His throat worked when he swallowed. "Look. I'm sorry. Robyn used to get after me for bossing her around, for always thinking I know the best way to do things. I guess I just, ah, fell back into old habits." Now he looked at her, and she saw the struggle in his pale green eyes. "I'll work on it. Okay?"

She swallowed hard, feeling the burn of a small victory. "Let's get those rooms and find a restaurant. You're right. I'm starving."

It was no big deal, she told herself. She could keep this casual.

She hoped.

BUT ONCE CASSIE was inside her motel room, which was saved from generic by whimsical touches of seashell and coral along the molding, she had trouble holding on to that blasé attitude. Her stomach jittered with more nerves than hunger, and she found herself staring into her suitcase, wishing she'd packed something sexier than pants and light businesslike shirts.

"This isn't a date," she told herself, and scowled into the mirror above the motel-issue dresser. "It's a convenience. He's here. I'm here. Why not eat together?"

But her reflection showed color riding high in her cheeks, and her pulse thrummed with anticipation as she quickly showered, blew her hair into soft, dry waves and pulled on clean underwear and her jeans. She left the business-like shirt untucked, and knotted it at her waist so a hint of her stomach showed when she moved.

Then she took a deep breath, gave herself a little pep talk, and let herself out of her room, locking the door securely at her back, even though she'd left nothing of value.

These days, she was more afraid of something being left *in* her room. The thought—and the reminder of danger—brought a faint shiver, but she pushed it aside as she marched to Varitek's door. She'd done what she could do for the night. She'd checked in on the progress the task force had made, and had finally gotten in touch with Maya, who insisted she was fine. There was little more to do now than wait for Varitek's people to finish with the fingerprints.

She might as well give herself permission to kick back for a few hours, so she took a deep breath, told herself this wasn't a real date, and knocked on the door to Varitek's unit.

But when the wood panel swung open and she saw his shower-slicked hair and caught the faintest hint of aftershave, her resolve crumbled against a wash of heat.

It sure as hell *felt* like a date.

HE WAS IN SERIOUS TROUBLE. Seth knew it as surely as he knew his own name the moment he saw her hair tumbling free across her shoulders. The soft blond waves made him itch to touch, to bury his fingers deep while he kissed her until they both ran out of air.

He cleared his throat. "The lady at the desk recommended a seafood place about a block away, right on the water."

Cassie nodded. "Sounds good. Want to walk?"

"Let's drive. Just in case." He couldn't shake

the suspicion that the killer had sent them to Florida on purpose, but why? What was back in Bear Claw that he didn't want them to see?

Or was there something in Florida he *wanted* them to see?

Not knowing, Seth kept his guard up as they walked to the rented SUV. Unable to stop himself, he opened the door for Cassie. She was one of the most capable women he'd ever met, yet he felt compelled to offer her a hand to help her inside.

He half expected her to throw the gesture back in his face. Instead, she took his hand, stepped close and looked up at him, and said, "Look, Varitek. I know this isn't really a date, but I think we'll both feel better if we get this out of the way."

Without warning, she stood up on her tiptoes and kissed him.

Surprise rocketed through him at the feel of her soft, lush lips against his, at the freshly showered, feminine scent of her rising up to surround him and cloud his brain. That was the only explanation for why he tightened his fingers on hers rather than pulling away, why he opened his mouth at the touch of her tongue rather than telling her this was a bad idea.

Or was it? Did he really need an explanation for something that felt this good?

Her flavor washed over him, into him, as their tongues met and mated. He looped their joined hands behind her back and pulled her closer, until their bodies were nearly aligned at thigh, hip and chest.

Where their first kiss had been a flameout of adrenaline and fighting madness, this was a meeting. A compromise. And the softness of it, the glory of it shimmered through him like the sunrise.

Heat rose, but it was a patient, binding heat that stayed warm when they eased apart.

Cassie's eyelids flickered then lifted, revealing now-confused blue eyes. She held his gaze for a long moment, during which he was acutely conscious of her rapid heartbeat and the rise and fall of her chest, which mirrored his own.

"Well," she finally said.

He shoved his hands in his pockets to keep himself from reaching for her again. "Yeah. Well."

She laughed nervously. "That didn't really clear the air, did it?"

"Nope." He jerked his head toward the rental. "Get in. I need to eat."

It was either that or sling her over his shoulder and carry her to his room.

THEY PASSED the short ride to the restaurant without speaking, but Cassie was getting used to Varitek's silences. When he had something to say, he said it. When he didn't, he was quiet. She liked that.

Actually, she was starting to like entirely too much about him, from the way he thought on the job to the way he'd admitted treating her differently and promised to work on it.

Not to mention the way he kissed.

She pressed her lips together, savoring the full, tender feeling of them. It had probably been a mistake to kiss him, but they'd both been wound tight and part of her had thought that might dispel the tension.

Wrong. If anything, it had made things worse, because now she knew that her memory of kissing him in the lab had been a hundred percent accurate. The man could kiss.

Hoo boy, could he kiss.

Her system had barely leveled by the time they pulled into the restaurant, which boasted an old boat purporting to be a prop from *The African Queen* out front and a kitschy collection of Bogart memorabilia and plastic fish hung near the door. She jumped out of the SUV before he could open the door and heard his faint chuckle as she led the way into the restaurant.

The kiss might have been her idea, but letting it go further wasn't part of the plan.

Once they'd placed their drink orders, she said, "I talked to Alissa. Turns out that two of Jasmine Gardner's friends positively ID'd a picture of Peter Dunbar. Apparently, he and Jasmine had sex and he snuck out on her—get this—the night before he was found dead."

Varitek nodded. "I've got my people processing Jasmine's bedroom right now. Maybe we'll get lucky."

Maybe not.

Cassie made a face that he already knew about the Jasmine-Peter connection, though she shouldn't have been surprised. Oddly enough, it didn't tick her off nearly as much as it would have a few days ago. Maybe she was mellowing, she thought, then was struck by a much less welcome thought.

What if she was caving on her own opinions to make Varitek like her more?

Suddenly annoyed, she straightened in her

chair and glared when the waiter leaned over to place her drink on the table. When he was gone, she said, "Alissa is sitting down with the girls right now to put together some sketches and a vehicle description. Apparently, Jasmine had been seeing someone else in the past week or so, someone older. She never introduced him to her friends, but one of the girls thinks she saw Jasmine get into his car the day before she was murdered."

Varitek didn't comment on whether or not he knew about the possible witness, because the waiter interrupted to give them the specials. Once he'd taken their orders and gone, Varitek said, "How do you figure Peter Dunbar and Jasmine Gardner fit in with the older skeleton, Marcia Pennington?"

"Marcia was practice, maybe." Cassie sipped her drink. They'd both ordered sodas without discussing the fact that they were, if not on duty, then on guard. "But if that's the case, where has he been for the past decade?

Killers don't just stop killing. Not usually. And then why bait us so we reopen the grave after so long? It doesn't make rational sense."

"Not the way you and I define rational, maybe." Varitek shrugged. "Killers have a tendency to redefine logic to suit themselves."

"True." They fell silent as their appetizers were delivered, but Cassie only picked at her food, because the pall of death had gathered over the small, dimly lit table for two.

Varitek deliberately dug into his appetizer. "Your neighbors seem like good people."

Cassie looked up, startled by the change in subject. "The McGlaughlins?"

"Didn't catch his name. Young guy with a baby face and a pump-action shotgun. Nearly put a big hole in me when I went to break down your door."

Though it was yet another reminder of the case and the danger, she grinned at the image and the subject change. "That's Dean. He's a sweetheart. I barely spoke to him and Mary for the first couple of months I lived in the house, but once little Eden came along, I just couldn't stay away." When he arched an eyebrow, she shrugged and laughed. "Go figure. I wouldn't have thought of myself as a baby person, either." When he didn't respond, she felt the heat of a faint blush in her cheeks and hoped he didn't think she was fishing. She quickly said, "So, you know that I live in a two-family. How about you? Something glass and chrome, with ten foot ceilings and double doors everywhere?"

She expected him to laugh. Instead, he grew pensive. Quiet, as though she'd struck a nerve when she was only looking for a safe topic of conversation. Finally, he said, "I have a good-sized house in a gated community outside of Denver. Stone floors, wood trim, big fireplace. That sort of thing. There's a studio at the back with great light and ventilation." His eyes darkened. "I keep meaning to drywall it and turn it into a gym, but it hasn't happened yet."

Cassie knew she shouldn't ask, but couldn't stop herself. "I take it the studio was your wife's?"

"It was supposed to be." He looked at her then, and his eyes held a weariness that tugged at her heart. He didn't even seem to notice the arrival of their entrées as he said, "We'd been fighting again, same old, same old. I thought if we changed the scenery, if Robyn had some-place that was hers, maybe she'd settle down and be happier."

He shifted in his chair while music drifted over from the club next door. A lone trumpet held a single note over the faint background hiss of the nearby sea.

"What did she think of that?" Cassie asked.

"About what you're probably imagining," he said dryly. "She loved the city, loved its pulse and its edge. Said I was trying to make her into a suburban housewife and she wouldn't stand for it."

"Couples fight," Cassie said, wishing she'd

never mentioned the house, never asked about the studio. "I'm sure she got over it."

"She never had the chance. The next day, she was attacked on her way home from the showing. I was supposed to be with her. I'd *promised* to be with her, but I got called to a scene." Varitek stared at his left hand, at the finger Cassie assumed had once worn a ring. "They'd planned it, of course, knowing I'd respond to the call. Hell, Trouper and I had been trying to get the Diablo brothers for nearly a year. We'd just put one of them away and were closing in on the other two. They'd made threats, of course, but I didn't listen."

As though suddenly remembering that he was hungry, Varitek lifted his fork and dug into his dinner with single-minded intensity, as though he was punishing the food, or maybe himself. The open window beside them let through the sound of the band next door, a melancholy collection of horns and strings with very little backbeat.

After a few minutes, Cassie decided she couldn't stand the strained silence anymore. She cleared her throat with a swallow of soda and said, "Listen, Varitek—"

"For God's sake," he snapped. "What do I have to do to get you to call me Seth?"

She jerked back from his anger, but told herself it wasn't aimed at her. It was the situation. The emotion. Something.

She stood, collected her purse and slapped a few bills on the table. "Come on, Seth. Let's take a walk."

He scowled at the money. "I'm paying, damn it."

When he reached for the bills she said, "Touch that and I'll break your fingers. Let's go."

Surprisingly, the empty threat worked. He drained his soda and stood, reminding her once again how much taller he was than she. How much stronger.

He followed her out onto the back terrace of the restaurant, then down onto the sand. When she paused near a string of colored lights to remove her shoes, he put a hand to the small of her back. "Let's get out of the light."

She knew he meant because they made better targets backlit by the restaurant. It was practicality, nothing more, but as the night closed around them and they walked down by the cloud-darkened water, the intimate isolation was undeniable.

They stayed side-by-side, shoulder-to-shoulder, but didn't touch. They walked slowly, their feet sinking into the soft sand, not walking for exercise or to get anywhere in particular, but because it was easier than sitting in a lit restaurant, facing each other.

Finally, Cassie said, "I know I've spent plenty of time telling you what you're doing wrong, what you need to change…but sometimes changing isn't the right answer. Sometimes, if you need to change that much it means that you're not with the right person."

"Sounds like you speak from experience."

Cassie tried to shrug off Seth's quiet sentence, but something about the darkness, the rush of the nearby water and the far away throb of music overcame some of her long-held barriers.

Or if they weren't overcome, they seemed less important, somehow.

"His name was Lee Adams. He was an instructor when I went for my M.S. in forensic chemistry and criminology. He was…" She paused, searching for the right words. "He was older than me by maybe eight or ten years, and everyone looked up to him because he'd been on the job. He was wounded on the streets and retired to teach—at least that was his story." She heard the bitterness in her voice and fought it, knowing she was just as much to blame as Lee had been.

He'd misled her, yes. But she'd allowed it.

"What was it, skiing accident?" Seth's dry question came out of the darkness and hit just the right chord within her.

Incredibly she was able to laugh about it. "Worse. It was an old tennis injury." She shook her head, knowing he couldn't see the motion. "I was completely and totally gullible. I even defended him to the other students. We started dating—" that sounded better than *I fell head over heels for him,* "—and moved in together after six months or so."

"And I'm guessing you fought." Seth paused in his walking step and turned to face her. "Look. I know you mean well, but there's a big difference between living with someone and being married. Marriage is permanent. There's no going back—the only option is to make it work, fights and all. And if you screw it up…" He spread his hands, a shadow of dark against light barely visible in the light from the beachside homes. "You're done. You only get one chance."

"We didn't fight," Cassie corrected him. "I changed so we wouldn't fight. I worked my butt off to be what he wanted, to keep the peace…until one day I looked in the mirror and didn't recognize myself anymore. I'd entered the program wanting to make it into the police academy, but I'd been spending so much time on Lee's things that I'd let my grades slip. Only one academy was willing to take a chance on me because of my science background and my test scores, but it would've meant leaving Lee and I'd gotten to the point that I couldn't even do that."

"Because you loved him," Seth said, his voice flat.

"No. Because I let him control me." Cassie fisted her hands at her sides and began walking again, back toward their restaurant and the sounds of a mournful trumpet solo. She was aware of Seth walking at her side, though she spoke as much to the memories as to him. "I listened when he told me I wouldn't be able to hack it at the academy, that I wouldn't be able to manage without him. I almost believed it when he said I should be grateful for the junior instructor's position he'd create for me. I could work with him, he said, but he really meant that I could work *for* him, just like I did at home."

Her feet dug deep, angry gouges in the sand. She wanted to run, but that would be giving Lee too much power, so she made herself walk while she continued the story. "I moved away from home because I was tired of my brothers protecting me, tired of them scaring off boys who wanted to date me. Then what did I do? I hooked up with someone a hundred times more controlling, and I didn't even see it. It took me eighteen months to get away from him, and another couple of years to really believe in myself, to be able to say that I'm good at my job." She forced a laugh that broke around the edges. "Maybe I say it too often or too loud, but I'm working on that. Slowly, but I'm working on it."

They had reached the halo of light surrounding their restaurant, but Seth laid a hand on her arm and stopped her just short of the lit patch of sand. "Hold on a minute."

She felt a shimmer of heat at his touch, a spark at the point of contact. "What?"

She expected him to continue the conversation, to argue that their situations were different, that he hadn't wanted to control his wife, he'd only wanted to keep her safe. She expected more heavy conversation, though her soul already felt like it was dragging from the weight of their not-really-a-date. She expected another fight, or maybe the silence he was so comfortable with.

She never expected him to hold out a hand as the band next door swung into something slow and bluesy, and say, "Dance with me? Just once before we go back inside."

Chapter Ten

They were quite a pair, Seth thought as she
took his hand. She was trying to prove her
worth to anyone who would listen, while he—

Hell, he didn't know what he was doing
anymore.

He held her close enough that he could catch
her scent on the sea air, but not as close as he
would have liked while they shuffled their feet
in the clinging sand. After a moment, she
sighed as though giving in to something, closed
the distance between them and tucked her head
into the hollow between his shoulder and jaw.

Warmth, a possessive and terrifying sort of
heat rose within him and he slid his arms
around her, holding her, until they were barely

swaying. The trumpeter swept a note high above the strings and held it as their mouths met and mated, their arms curled around each other and held on.

The kiss started out soft, almost experimental, as though neither of them quite believed in the heat. But the fire rose quickly, scorching him, consuming him, bringing them closer and closer together until he wasn't sure where his flesh ended and hers began. He dragged his mouth to the hollow behind her ear and sifted his fingers through the long waves of her hair.

Her fingers dug into his back, then clutched in his shirt to pull it up and out of his waistband. Then her hands were beneath the cloth, stroking his back, his ribs. Everywhere she touched, small embers ignited, a chain reaction of pleasure that nearly drove him mad.

He growled and kissed her again, a deep, wet, searching kiss that had her murmuring acceptance and crowding closer. Frustrated by the layers of clothing that separated them, he slid his hands down to span her waist.

And found it bare already.

The tails of her shirt were untied, granting him access to the warm, taut skin beneath. He slid his hand up, then higher still until he could—

A wolf whistle drowned out the last dying notes of the trumpet, and a man's voice shouted, "Woo-hoo! You go, dude!" A babble of voices seconded the suggestion.

Seth cursed and tightened his hold on Cassie when she would have pulled away. He turned and glared at the group of college-age kids who were leaning on one another as they staggered up the beach to God only knew where. But he was just as angry at himself.

If the drunken revelers had managed to get the drop on him, their killer could have done the same at any damned moment.

Cassie tugged at his arm. "We should go."

He wasn't sure whether she meant because of the young men, who continued to shout uncreative suggestions, because of the threat of danger, or because their night was over. Knowing she was right on all three counts, he scooped her shoes from the sand, shook them out and offered them to her. She pulled the sneakers on, and they slipped around the side of the restaurant, not wanting to walk through the dining area and be reminded of their earlier awkward conversation or too-quick departure.

When she stumbled in the darkness, he took her hand for support and didn't let go once they were back in the light. Heat thrummed from the point of contact, undimmed by the cool air moving beneath his untucked shirt. Instead of fading, the sensual excitement only climbed as he checked beneath the SUV—just in case— and helped Cassie into the passenger seat.

When he took the driver's seat and started the engine, she sat quietly, but when he placed his hand on the console between them, she curled her fingers around his in a signal of agreement.

Acceptance.

When he parked at the motel, amidst the multicolored lights given off by the stained-glass lampshades, she waited for him to get her door and help her down, a rare concession for a woman he knew damn well could be as tough as any man on the job.

But she was all woman as she walked to her door, stopped, turned back—

And held out a hand in invitation.

HE THOUGHT ABOUT ARGUING. Cassie could see it in his eyes, feel it in her soul. But the arguments didn't seem to matter as much anymore. Not after their walk on the beach.

Not after that dance they'd shared at the edge between darkness and light.

So he took her hand without a word, without the obligatory *are you sure?* He waited while she unlocked the door and quickly checked the room, just in case.

All the while, she was aware of him

watching her. Aware of the blood thrumming just below the surface of her skin, making the brush of her clothes nearly unbearable.

When she was sure there had been nobody in her room, that there was nobody in the closet, no ticking device beneath the bed, she locked the door behind them both, clicked off the light and turned toward him.

The outdoor light filtered through the curtains, splashing them with the soft, aching romance of stained glass. Both of them were breathing fast, as though they'd run to reach the place they'd gotten to.

And maybe, in a way, they had.

Once she was facing him, with no distractions to blunt the power of his presence, she faltered. Her pulse stuttered at the intensity of his eyes, at the sheer size of him.

Nerves were a sudden, unwelcome friend.

"I'm sure of this," he said, surprising her because there was no question in his voice, no hesitation. "I don't know what's going to come of it, but this is right for me." He swallowed hard. "It's time for me to stop running in place, time to finish turning the studio into a gym and move on."

The darkness cloaked them in intimacy, and a bird called outside, sounding like the last, fading note of a single trumpet. That memory, coupled with the need she had been trying to avoid for days—maybe months—sent Cassie forward until she and Seth were almost touching.

She looked up into his eyes and feared he would see the vulnerability when she said, "I gave Lee too much power over me even after I left him. I'm ready to stop doing that."

She wondered if he noticed that neither of them mentioned the other, neither of them mentioned wanting to be together, wanting to stay together. Maybe that was implied.

Maybe it simply wasn't time for that.

They closed the final distance between them, meeting halfway as equals, as partners, and she found herself wishing they hadn't been interrupted on the beach. There, the fire had flared high between them, blunting rational thought and giving them the excuses. *It was the heat of the moment. It was just sex.*

But as their lips touched, hesitated and held, she knew neither of those excuses rang true anymore. There was heat, yes. Excitement warmed her, spread through her, igniting chain reactions deep inside as he slanted his mouth across hers and sought entry. There was charged electricity as he slid his big arms around her, cupping her bare waist beneath the untied shirt and sliding his thumbs to either side of her stomach, where want thrummed just beneath the skin.

But this wasn't the heat of the moment anymore. This was an acknowledged decision, one that Cassie reinforced by opening her mouth to him, tangling her tongue with his and sliding her hands beneath his shirt and up his chest, where a faint dusting of hair was soft contrast to the hard muscle beneath. *Yes,* her hands and her mouth said wordlessly, *I will be your lover tonight.*

The heat rose higher as his fingers clamped on her denim-covered hips and she pulled his shirt off, leaving him gloriously bare above. She slid her hands up across the hardness of his biceps and the width of his shoulders, reveling in the feel of him, the strength of him. He muttered a dark promise and crowded her backward. She expected to feel the soft mattress at her knees.

Instead, he pressed her against the wall and kissed her until her heart fought to break free of her rib cage. He slid his hands down to her thighs, just above her knees, and lifted her in one smooth, powerful move. Suddenly, their mouths and hips were perfectly aligned and her legs formed a pocket for him, allowing him to step forward and into her so his lower body held her aloft, allowing his hands freedom to roam.

His strength should have made her feel small and weak, but instead it made her feel powerful. Alive.

Greedy for more.

She went to work on his belt and the snap and zipper beneath, while their mouths met over and over again, giving and taking, then taking again. He undid the last few buttons on her shirt and unfastened the front-clip bra beneath. For an instant, she wished it had been dark lace rather than plain cotton, but his groan when he touched her, cupped her, caressed her, told her that dark lace would have been wasted on him.

It was the woman beneath who mattered.

That realization warmed her, reassured her, and she pushed his pants down over his hips, where they snagged on her legs and the place he had her pressed to the wall.

"Allow me," he said between quick, deep breaths and long, slow kisses. And before she could brace her-self, he'd scooped her up, turned away from the wall and moved to the dresser.

Seeing his intent, and approving with a startled flash of heat, she swept her arm across the surface, sending shells and coral flying. He propped her on the waist-high wood surface and kissed her, then stepped into the vee between her legs.

"Too many clothes," she said when the kiss broke, and pushed him away so she could slide off the dresser.

Leaving her shirt and bra looped over her shoulders, she wriggled out of her pants, panties and shoes while he shrugged out of his pants, and went back for his wallet. He held up a single packet. "I've only got one condom. We'll have to make it worthwhile."

She grinned and boosted herself back onto the dresser. "Bring it on."

She didn't mention that she had a couple of con-doms in her overnight bag, packed because…hell, she didn't know what she'd been thinking, but wasn't it lucky that she had?

He sheathed himself and moved to face her. Their bodies were perfectly aligned, only touching where he placed his hands on her thighs and she pressed her palms against the hard planes of his chest. The light from outdoors gleamed down on them, frosting the wide line of his shoulders with blue and green, as though they were underwater.

Her heart pounded up into her throat when he leaned forward to kiss her, and stepped into her, until he was pressed at the entrance to her body, to her heart.

No, she told herself, even as she lifted her hands to frame his face as they kissed. Not her heart. Her heart was safe. She would make sure of that.

But as he slid his hands behind her, that second excuse flitted through her mind. *It's just sex.*

She told herself that as he eased himself into

her, filling her, stretching her until she felt as though it should have hurt but didn't. She told herself it was just sex when her heart expanded in her chest, filling her to bursting, and he began to move within her, they began to move together.

She told herself it was just sex as the pleasure coiled within her, hard and ready and wanting. She dug her fingernails into his shoulders and closed her eyes, unable to watch the exquisite power of his face, the way his eyes had darkened in the blue-green light, the way they suddenly saw inside her.

Saw *her.*

"Look at me," he ordered. *"Look at me."*

She did, because she was helpless to do otherwise as the tidal wave ripped through her. She looked at him just in time to see him climax, to see the power of his pleasure and feel it deep inside her body.

Inside her heart.

And in that moment, in that hesitating heartbeat before she came a second time, she knew the final, awesome, terrifying truth.

It wasn't just sex.

It was something much bigger.

WOW, SETH THOUGHT unimaginatively. Just wow.

And oh, boy, was he in trouble.

After a long moment of leaning into Cassie, leaning against her, he righted himself on rubbery legs, scooped her up and deposited her on the bed. Then he made a vague gesture toward the bathroom, and escaped.

He took care of the condom, then ran cold water into the basin and splashed his face, his chest, the back of his neck, anywhere he could reach that might do the trick. He wasn't trying to wash her away, though.

He was trying to pull himself the hell together.

He hadn't expected this any more than he'd expect to climb out of bed one morning and find a tiger in his bathroom. It was that huge.

He'd gone into her arms expecting physical satisfaction. He'd gotten it, all right, but he'd gotten something else, as well. Emotion. And Seth couldn't afford to do emotion.

Not this time. Not with this woman. He'd made that mistake before, confusing good sex with love. Robyn had been a wonderful woman, but not his match. She and Cassie were similar in that way.

He grabbed a towel and scrubbed his face dry, trying to erase the faint, unaccountable sting of guilt. "We didn't promise each other anything," he said aloud, but quietly enough so Cassie wouldn't hear.

In fact, he'd been careful not to promise.

There was a soft knock on the bathroom door. "Seth? You okay?"

He knotted the towel around his hips and opened the door to find Cassie on the other side. She had buttoned her shirt, but her long, bare legs stretched out below, making him wonder what she had on underneath.

She took a breath. "This doesn't have to be weird, okay?" She held out a hand. "Come back to bed. I'll be disappointed if you run."

He took her hand, and held it, waiting until she looked up at him. "I can't promise anything."

"I'm not asking you to. Just come back to bed."

So he followed her gentle urging and climbed between the covers with her. He cuddled her close because they both seemed to need it. During the remainder of the night, he made full use of the two condoms she produced from her overnight bag, because they both wanted it. But even as he tried to armor his heart against the softer emotions she brought out in him, he realized that he should have promised her something, after all.

He should have promised her that their relationship would end when the case did.

He was done with forever.

EARLY THE NEXT MORNING, Cassie felt the bed shift as Seth rolled away from her and stood.

She kept her eyes shut, because she wasn't at her best at haven't-had-coffee-yet o'clock in the morning. And because she was a wimp. She didn't want to do the awkward morning-after thing.

She'd asked him to stay and he had stayed. That should be enough for now. He was finding his way out of the grief of a marriage that had ended before he could fix it. She was finally ready to try holding her own against a man with opinions as strong as her own. They could figure the rest out together.

At least that was what she told herself. But when he leaned over the bed dressed in last night's clothes, and kissed her on the cheek, she had to force herself not to move, not to grab onto him and cling. That was the needy part of her. The part that had allowed Lee to manipulate her into his notion of love. The part that she refused to bring into her relationship with Seth.

So she kept still and listened to him leave

the room and shut the door. His footsteps sounded along the walkway outside, followed by the sound of a key in the lock of his room.

Once the door shut again and he was in his room, she sat up slowly, sensually, feeling the pull of long-unused muscles and the gut-deep satisfaction of having been well loved. She gave herself a moment to savor the sensations and the memories, then rose and headed for the shower.

The ring of her cell phone brought her up short. She crossed the room, dug the unit out of her crumpled jeans, and flipped it open. "Hello?"

"We've got a suspect," Alissa's voice said, sharp with satisfaction. "The witnesses remembered enough about the vehicle they saw to put us on track, and the sketch I developed from them matches the owner. Denver Lyttle. No rap sheet, but he was dishonorably discharged from the military two years ago after being trained as—get this—an explosives expert."

"Wow. I—wow!" Cassie faltered as reality made a quick return. The previous night notwithstanding, she wasn't in Florida for a romantic getaway. She and Seth were chasing a murderer. At least they had been. It sounded like the case was breaking open without them. She swallowed a bubble of professional disappointment and said, "Great work, Lissa! Is Lyttle in custody?"

"Tucker just picked him up. They'll be here any minute."

Through the thin wall, Cassie heard Seth's phone ring, heard the deep, dark rumble of his voice answering.

"Cass? You there?" Alissa demanded.

Cassie yanked her attention back to her friend. "Sorry. I'm here. Seth and I are just about to head over to Fitz's place. Assuming that the fingerprints were fakes—which seems reasonable if our guy is in custody already—we'll ask Fitz how he's connected to Denver Lyttle."

She tried to keep the disappointment out of

her voice at the idea of doing mop-up work. She should be thrilled to hear that the Bear Claw cops had caught a solid suspect.

So why wasn't she?

"Seth?" Alissa's voice caught a teasing edge. "You two are on a first name basis now?"

Cassie was grateful for the knock on her door. "Look, I've got to go. I'll call you later to see how Lyttle's interrogation went." She flipped the phone shut and blew out a breath, unable to explain the sudden churning in her stomach.

The knock came again. "You ready?"

"In a minute," she called, damning the heat that touched her core at the sound of his voice. "I'll meet you by the car."

Within five minutes she was dressed and packed for the flight home, but her system still wasn't level. She was churned up by the thought that Alissa and the others had nabbed a solid suspect. But why was it such a big deal? Was she so insecure that she needed to be in on the collar? Muttering, she slung her overnight bag over her shoulder, put her hand to the doorknob leading out, and then paused and turned back to the room.

It was the same room she'd walked into the evening before, the same plain furniture, the same coral and shell accents. But it carried memories now. Memories of Seth pressing her against the wall and taking her under with his kiss. Memories of lovemaking on the dresser. In the bed. Memories of the two of them.

And she got it.

She wasn't upset that the others might have caught the murderer without her. She was bothered that with the case closed, she would lose her new partner. Seth would head back to the Denver field office and she'd go back to being the least popular member of the Bear Claw P.D.

"Don't be silly," she told herself. They were grown-ups with cars, e-mail and telephones. The end of the case didn't mean the end of their…whatever it was. In fact, it would probably be easier for them to get to know each other from neutral corners, as it were.

Cheered, she pushed through the door and closed it behind her, feeling only a twinge of freshly minted nostalgia at the sight of the stained-glass lamps outside.

This wasn't the end. It was a beginning.

She hoped.

WHEN CASSIE climbed into the rented SUV, Seth handed her a cardboard cup of coffee and a grocery store pastry, both courtesy of the motel management. "Did Alissa update you on the suspect?"

He noticed that she avoided his eyes as she accepted the food and drink. She took a sip of the coffee, then another, longer sip, and sighed. "Thank God. Caffeine." Then she glanced at him and nodded. "Yep. Denver Lyttle. The connection sounds pretty solid, though we'll want better evidence than just witness reports of a vehicle and a man."

"True enough," Seth agreed. Eyewitnesses were notoriously unreliable. Hard evidence wasn't. He started the engine, referred to the directions and headed them towards Key Lobo and Fitz's place. Then he lowered his voice and said, "Look, Cassie. I wanted to talk to you about—"

She held up a hand to stop him. "Wait." When he paused, she tucked her coffee cup into the dashboard holder and clasped her hands together as though concentrating on picking just the right words. "I know we need to talk about what happened. But not now, okay? We're on duty and I don't think it's appropriate. Alissa and Tucker have had to draw some pretty strict lines between work and…not work. I think we should try to do the same."

Though he was uncomfortable with the way she'd compared the two of them to the newly engaged couple, Seth knew she was right. There was only so far they could blur the lines without stepping over.

So he nodded. "Fine. We'll talk on the flight home. For now, we'll concentrate on Fitz. My people finished with the fingerprints, and sure enough, they were laid in synthetic oil, inconsistent with a human fingerprint. Ergo, they're fake. But why? We'll need to ask Fitz about this Denver Lyttle character. There should be some connection if Lyttle's our man."

They talked sporadically about the case over the twenty minutes it took to reach Key Lobo and park on the dead-end street where Fitz lived. His was the only house on the street, with a generous screening of trees and shrubs separating him from the nearest neighbors, giving the cul de sac a sense of privacy. There was a late-model sedan in the cement driveway of the single-level waterfront bungalow, and a small boat bobbed at a dock beyond.

Seth opened his door and jumped down from the SUV. "Looks like a pretty sweet retirement setup to me."

Cassie joined him on the short walkway

leading to Fitz's house. "I prefer gardens over all this cement."

The comment brought an image to his mind, one of Cassie kneeling in a freshly turned garden, surrounded by plants and a white picket fence. That was what she wanted, he knew. That, plus a loving husband and a baby to complete the picture. Not someone like him, with a half-finished gym at the back of his house and no intentions of remarrying.

"Varitek?" She raised an eyebrow. "You okay?"

He knew she'd deliberately used his last name to emphasize the professional distance. He nodded curtly. "Let's go."

Aware that she'd slipped her weapon from her mid-back holster, he walked to the door and knocked, not expecting a problem, but braced for one nonetheless.

The knock echoed through the house. A bird of some sort screeched in protest, and he heard a man's voice curse over the background chatter of a television news program. Footsteps approached, quick and measured, sounding nothing like an old man's stride. Then the door opened and Fitzroy O'Malley stood in the gap looking ten years younger than he had the last time Varitek had seen him.

Fitz was five-ten and built like a bulldog, with close-cropped salt-and-pepper hair and muddy brown eyes nearly lost amidst the crow's feet of years spent outdoors. Seth remembered from previous jobs in Bear Claw that Fitz and Chief Parry had looked like bookends when they stood opposite each other, both tough and weathered and not about to put up with any garbage from the public, the perps, or the other cops.

The former evidence specialist still looked like a bulldog, but now he looked like a tan, well-fed, well-rested bulldog.

One that narrowed its eyes and bared its teeth at the intruders on his front step.

"Varitek." The name wasn't quite a greeting.

Fitz's eyes slid over to Cassie. "That'd make you Dumont. The one nobody likes." He returned his attention to Seth. "I had a call that you were on your way."

Seth supposed he should have expected that the information would leak within the Bear Claw P.D., but he knew from experience that Fitz preferred straight talk to playing nice, so he said, "Consider yourself lucky that you've moved down on our suspect list. Since we're here, how about you tell us who would want to implicate you in a pair of murders, and how you know Denver Lyttle."

Fitz snorted and glanced at Cassie. "You two want to come inside, or does the new forensics department recommend front porch interrogations?"

Cassie bristled and swung around so she fully faced the door, away from her backup position. "Listen, you—"

A shot split the air.

Fitz lurched back into the house, clutching his chest.

And everything went to hell.

Chapter Eleven

"Everybody down!" Cassie shouted. She flinched when a second shot slammed into the vinyl siding beside her head. She grabbed Seth, or he grabbed her, she wasn't quite sure, and they lunged into the house together.

Seth kicked the door shut as a third shot blasted clean through the panel and buried itself in a new-looking sofa.

Cassie smelled blood, looked down and saw the red liquid leaking from between the fingers Fitz had clamped to his chest.

He needed help. Fast.

A fourth shot took out the window above her head as she shouted, "I'll call it in and deal with Fitz. Cover us!" She ducked down and crab-walked toward the phone while Seth pulled his weapon and edged an eye above the windowsill, trying to get a bead on the gunman.

She called 911 and gave the address, then crouched down beneath the hallway table to check Fitz's wound.

Seth fired off a couple of rounds and the gunman answered with a shot that shattered a water glass on the table over her head. Cassie clenched her teeth and forced her fingers not to shake as she tugged the older man's hand away from his bloody chest.

She trusted Seth to protect her.

The bullet had gone in higher than she'd thought, which was good, because it meant muscle and bone damage rather than lung and heart. She hoped so, because she had a few new questions to ask Fitz. Not seeing an obvious exit wound, she put the older man's hands back on his chest, covered them with her own, and pressed down, trying to stop the blood.

Seth cursed as three more shots whistled through the broken window near his head. "The bastard's hiding behind our rental. Must've been following us."

Cassie glanced at Fitz, who had gone gray-white. "Or else he was waiting for us."

Her voice sounded suddenly loud in the absence of gunshots. Silence descended on the scene, broken only by Fitz's labored breathing and the crackle of shattered glass.

Then, faded by distance, they heard sirens.

"Cavalry's coming," Seth said, "and our guy rabbited. Stay here, I'll be back." He stood quickly, and slipped out the door before Cassie could tell him not to go.

Which was just as well. It had been her idea for them to keep their personal and professional interactions separate. Professionally, he had to go after the gunman, had to catch the guy before someone else got hurt.

Personally, she wanted him to stay the hell safe.

She cursed under her breath and glared at Fitz. "If anything happens to him…" Then she trailed off, because the older man was close to unconscious.

Anxiety kicked in. She was no doctor. What if the bullet had gone in high and ricocheted around? He could die on her.

She pinched him on the leg. "Fitz! Hey, O'Malley, wake up. Do you hear me? Stay awake. The ambulance will be here any minute." The sirens still sounded far away, but they were growing louder by the moment. She hoped to hell Seth had called in his position on his cell phone so he could rendezvous with backup.

The thought of him taking on the gunman solo sent a shiver down her spine, but she told herself he was trained and capable. He'd be fine.

Please, let him be fine.

She shouted in Fitz's ear again, and this time the older man's eyes eased open and he focused on her face. "They said you like to yell. Guess they were right."

His voice wasn't strong, but at least he was lucid. She was aware of the sirens growing louder, of the time ticking away and the blood leaking from beneath their layered hands.

"Look, Fitz," she said urgently, "I know we don't know each other and we probably wouldn't like each other if we did, but I need you to tell me the truth, okay?"

His breathing was shallow and pained, but he managed to say, "New-fangled cops like you don't know the truth unless your computer tells it to you."

She ignored that and asked, "Who told you we were on our way here?"

His eyes narrowed. "Nobody."

"Baloney. You were expecting us. Who told you?" The evidence still pointed toward someone with police department connections. If they could get a name—

"Some new rookie," Fitz wheezed. "Didn't

know him. Said he was calling on behalf of one of the older detectives."

"His name," Cassie pressed. "What was his name?"

"Don't remember. Something odd, like a girl's name. I think I wrote it down." He smiled weakly, strength fading. "I still take notes when I talk on the phone. Can't seem to break the habit."

When his eyelids fluttered, Cassie raised her voice. "Fitz, stay with me. Do you know Denver Lyttle?" She briefly sketched what Alissa had told her of the suspect's history. "Do you know why he would want to frame you for the murder?"

But even as Fitz shook his head in the negative, she realized that there was a new question to answer. If Lyttle was in custody, how could they account for the gunman?

Either he'd hired a hit to track them all the way to Florida.

Or their prime suspect was innocent.

She cursed as she heard the rescue vehicles pull into the dead-end street, heard the shouts of cops being deployed. She raised her voice and shouted, "The shooter's gone. Special Agent Varitek is in pursuit. The house is clear."

Still, it took the cops several minutes to secure the scene before the paramedics could push through. Once they were working to stabilize Fitz, Cassie stood aside, acutely aware that Seth hadn't returned and none of the cops knew where he was. He hadn't called for backup.

She clenched her fists at her sides, told herself not to panic, told herself he was fine, but the worry beat in her chest alongside her heart, relentless and unceasing.

The paramedics were preparing to lift Fitz into the ambulance when she suddenly broke from her paralysis. "Wait!" She rushed outside and pushed the medical personnel aside. "Wait. Can he talk?"

"He shouldn't," said one paramedic, a sturdy

woman in her late thirties. But Fitz pushed the oxygen mask aside and gestured for her to talk.

"Does the name Marcia Pennington ring a bell?" she asked, naming the young woman whose remains they'd discovered in the canyon. "Missing person eight years ago, disappeared from the Tyngsboro area."

Fitz shook his head in the negative, but she thought she caught a flicker of recognition in his expression.

Knowing her time was running out, she said, "Last one. Who would want you framed for murder?"

At that, his lips twitched. His breathing remained shallow, but he forced the words. "Sweet cheeks, you spend as long on the job as I did and there'll be a line of people wanting to kill you or frame you or both."

With that, he pulled the oxygen mask into place and gestured for the paramedics to take him.

"Get anything useful out of old Fitz?" a deep voice said behind her.

Cassie squeaked and spun, heart suddenly pounding in her ears, in her chest. "Seth!"

His weapon was holstered and a faint sheen of sweat dampened his short hair, though his face and neck looked rubbed-dry.

Cassie didn't think it through, didn't stop to worry about the other cops, didn't stop to think about the line between personal and professional.

She simply closed the distance between them, wrapped her arms around his waist and laid her cheek against his chest. "I'm glad you're okay."

He stood frozen for a moment before his hands lifted. She felt them hover above her shoulders for a heartbeat, as though he wanted to ease her away. Then he inhaled a deep breath, exhaled on a sigh, and wrapped his arms around her. "Me, too."

They clung together for a minute, then he

squeezed her tight and they parted. Ignoring the stares and smirks of the assembled cops, he said, "The bastard got away and I didn't even get a good look at him. You get anything from Fitz?"

"Not really," she said, frustrated with the questioning, and the sense that he had re-membered something about Marcia Penning-ton and hadn't told her. He hadn't wanted to talk about his enemies, either. All she'd needed was something to use as a starting point. A name, a—

Wait. A name.

"Hang on." She turned and headed back into the house. The Key Lobo cops didn't follow, but Seth did, and she gave him credit for only wincing slightly when she ripped the top sheet off the message pad beside Fitz's phone, messing with the locals' crime scene. She folded the note, hid it in her palm and gestured him out of the house.

They quickly traded the necessary information, put the Key Lobo cops in contact with Chief Parry, and hit the road in a cab, since the rented, bullet-dinged SUV had been impounded as evidence. Once they were moving, she unfolded the sheet of paper and read the name aloud.

Anna Susie.

Who the hell was that?

THE PLANNER'S CALL came too soon, before the hunter was fully braced for it, before he was ready to admit that he had failed to bag his prey.

"It's all a matter of territory," he said into the cell phone, skipping the pleasantries. "I don't like it here. It's too crowded. There are too many people, too many witnesses. Everything is so close together. There aren't any good hiding spaces, and I had to work during the daylight. You know I hate the daylight."

True hunters stalk at night, his father had told him, and they had donned army surplus night-vision goggles and tracked their targets in the dark.

Remembering it, the hunter stroked the stock of the gun he had purchased from a legitimate—but bribable—pawnbroker. It wasn't the best long-gun in the world, as its crooked sights had proven, but still, he loved the feel of a hunting rifle.

So many memories.

"In other words, you failed," the planner said, voice stiff with disapproval.

"I got the old man." The hunter looked around at the place he'd gone to ground, an unlocked boathouse he'd scouted out prior to his ambush. "The information was good. They showed up like you said they would. But the situation wasn't optimal."

The fact was he'd missed. That galled him. Crooked sights or no, he shouldn't have missed. Sluggish anger stirred in his gut, but still, he stroked the rifle butt, loving the feel of the soft, slick wood.

He wouldn't miss again.

"They could be at the hospital," he said. "I can find out which one and—"

"No," the planner interrupted. "Too public. You missed your chance. Come home."

Though moments earlier he'd been lamenting the discomfort of being outside his territory, the hunter frowned. "Let me do it here. Give me another chance. I know I can do it."

"I said come home, son." The voice took on an edge of steel, of irritation. "I have something else planned for you."

The other man cut the connection without waiting for assent, leaving the hunter to sit in silence for a moment, while restless waves lapped at the edges of the boathouse and his gut churned with resentment. "You can't tell me what to do," he hissed. "You're not my father." In the hunter's mind, the planner's voice said *son*, as it had a thousand times, only this time the word grated on his nerves and made him shout, "You're not my father!"

The words bounced off the boathouse walls and reflected off the water like little waves. Tiny echoes. *You're not my father. Not my father. My father. Father.*

His father was dead.

Gunshots echoed in the hunter's brain, alongside the howl of a hound dog and a boy's startled scream as he fell into the memory.

He hadn't meant to do it. The gun had taken on a life of its own, or maybe his hands had made the choice. He'd been nearly a grown man, all awkward arms and legs and too-big feet. One minute they had been tracking a magnificent buck in silence, the tension of their latest argument humming in the air between them, and in the next, he had stepped outside his sire's footprints.

A twig snapped, gunshot loud, and their prey bolted deeper into the forest. The stag gave them a last, mocking glimpse of its bobbing white tail and wide, lofty rack.

And was gone.

His father spun, big and angry in night-vision goggles and winter layers. "Christ, boy, can't you do anything right?" He advanced on the hunter, who had been called Nevada back then. The hunting dog slunk at the big man's heels, hackles raised, sensing a fight. "I told you to get your mind off that slut and focus on your footing."

"I wasn't thinking about her, Dad, honest!" Nevada fell back a few paces and held up his hands in the surrender his father usually demanded. But then a flare of defiance guttered in his chest, the sort of rebellion that had gotten him in trouble before. He took a step forward. "And she's not a slut!"

"Of course she is. They all are, even your mother. Hell, she's probably banging some poor guy right now." The big man's fingers touched his belt. "We'll see about that."

"She's not my mother," Nevada shouted back, knowing his real mother had left them years ago. The woman his father lived with now, Marie, was no blood of his. "She's just some skank you picked up in a bar."

And though the old man had called Marie much worse, his features twisted with rage and he grabbed for his belt buckle. "Don't you dare say such things about your mother! She was a good woman, smarter than both of us put together."

Yeah, Nevada thought. *My real mother got away from you.*

And it was in that moment that he finally knew he was as smart as his mother, smart enough to get free.

His hands took over, acting without conscious thought. His father tossed his hunting rifle aside and advanced, yanking the heavy belt out of its loops with a too-familiar whistling *crack.*

"Time to teach you a lesson," Nevada said, mo-ments before his father's voice said the words. The boy raised the rifle.

And fired point-blank.

The shot echoed in his mind, in his ears, reverberating in his head until he jolted and realized it wasn't the memory anymore. The tide had come up within the boathouse, floating a tethered metal hook, which banged against the covered dock. *Bang. Bang. Bang.*

That was how many shots he'd fired into his father. Three. Then one into the hunting dog that used to sit and watch, panting and grinning, while the old man took his strap to Nevada. Or maybe his fists. A wooden bat once or twice.

Damn dog.

The hunter flexed his fingers, which creaked stiffly. How long had he been sitting in the boathouse? No matter, it was time to move on. Time to return home as he had been commanded. And though the planner wasn't his father, wasn't any blood kin at all, the older man had kept the hunter safe and let him do his work.

He thought about the women, about their

chiding fingertips and that flashy belly button ring that had reminded him of—what? He didn't even remember anymore. The individual deaths seemed less important than the whole.

That long-ago afternoon he'd walked out of the forest, alone and spattered with blood. He'd expected Marie to scream, to call the cops, to turn him in. And maybe part of him had wanted that.

Instead, she had cleaned him up and spread her legs for him. If he was man enough to take care of that bastard father of his, she'd said, he was man enough for her.

They had fled the state together, and he'd become a man overnight, thanks to his height and a fake ID. They had kept moving, while he grew up and learned how to survive. But of all the lessons she'd taught him before he killed her, that first lesson was the most important.

His father was right. Women were sluts.

All of them.

The hook banged on the boathouse wall in counterpoint to the words. *All of them. All of them. All of them.*

It was nearly noon before he kissed the crooked-sighted rifle and dropped it in the water. Then he emerged from the boathouse, shook off the strange lethargy that weighted his limbs and hiked out to a nearby strip mall.

The planner was right. It was time to go home.

His prey was waiting for him.

Chapter Twelve

The flight home sat on the tarmac for almost an hour, delayed by thunderstorms. Seth and Cassie pondered the name on Fitz's telephone pad. Anna Susie.

"I'm pretty sure Fitz said the caller was a man." Cassie frowned, a faint wrinkle gathering between her eyebrows. "A male rookie cop named Anna? I don't think so."

"Maybe Fitz got the name wrong," Seth said, shifting in his seat when their arms pressed together and he found it entirely too comfortable.

They hadn't yet discussed their relationship. Maybe he was being a coward by not forcing the issue right then, but they had work to do.

A murderer to catch before he killed again.

There were too many questions and not enough answers. Why send them to Florida? If the killer was trying to implicate Fitz, why call and warn him that they were coming to question him about the murders?

Seth cursed. "We need more data."

"Unfortunately, it seems like we know less by the minute." Cassie frowned. "Alissa said the Denver Lyttle lead petered out. Never mind the fact that he clearly wasn't in Florida yesterday, he had solid alibis for two of the important time periods. We're talking security tapes from the store where he works—pretty solid evidence."

"That's the problem with eyewitnesses," Seth grumbled, feeling the first tendrils of a headache build. He was tired and churned up, jumbled between the need to work the case and the need to set things straight with Cassie.

He was hyperaware of her motions as she settled back in her first-class seat and gave a jaw-cracking yawn. Her arm brushed against his and their knees touched. The innocent contact sent a sizzle of warmth into his chest, reminding him of what they'd done the night before. What they'd become.

Lovers.

The word carried too much responsibility, too many expectations that he wouldn't be able to meet. She'd be better off with someone other than him, someone who could make the promises she deserved.

He shifted in his seat and turned to her. "Look, Cassie. I really think we should," *talk*, he'd meant to say, but didn't bother because she was fast asleep.

He muttered a curse but didn't wake her, because neither of them had slept much the night before, and because he wasn't sure what he wanted to say. Or rather, he knew what he *ought* to say, but was having problems saying it aloud.

He stared at her for a long moment, at the

way her long lashes—a shade darker than her hair—lay on her cheeks, making her look softer. More vulnerable.

Hollowness ached in his chest at the thought of her being hurt. By the killer.

By him.

The pilot announced that they'd begin takeoff preparation in twenty minutes. That gave Seth plenty of time to make a call.

Before he could question the urge, he dialed a familiar number, one he hadn't called nearly enough lately.

"Hello?"

"CeeCee, it's me." He kept his voice pitched low, not wanting to wake Cassie. Then, realizing the privacy was an illusion, he said, "Hang on a minute."

He unbuckled his seat belt, stood and crab-walked through the front of the first class section, where there was a small alcove near the lavatories. He pulled out one of the folding jump-seats the flight attendants used during takeoff and landing, and sat. "Okay. I'm back. How are you?"

"We're fine. What's wrong? Where are you?"

Seth chuckled at the edge in his sister's voice, the maternal protectiveness she'd worn like a badge ever since that first day their mother had said, *CeeCee, you're in charge of your little brother. Keep him out of trouble.*

"I'm on my way home from Florida and I'm fine." He leaned his head back against the airplane bulkhead. "I just…hell, I don't know."

Ever-practical, solid CeeCee said, "The last time I heard that tone of voice, you'd bought the Denver house and were afraid to tell Robyn about it."

"This is nothing like—" He paused. "Okay, maybe it is. I've gotten myself into something and I'm not sure how to get out without hurting someone."

There was a pause. He couldn't hear anything in the background, which meant that CeeCee's husband and kids were off somewhere else, because Lord knew, they weren't a quiet bunch. Then she said, "This isn't about your work, is it?" And there was a new, softer note in her voice.

"No."

"I'm glad," she said simply. "It's time. Robyn would want you to move on and be happy."

"I'm perfectly happy," he argued, "and you're not listening to me. I'm not starting something. I'm trying to figure out how to end it without hurting the woman in question."

"What's her name?"

He sighed. "Cassie."

"And what's the matter with her? She have a criminal record? Antisocial tendencies? Bad breath?"

He snorted. "No. None of those things."

"Then why end it? You don't love her?"

"I barely know her!" The response rang false, but Seth ignored the twinge and said, "It's not fair to her. She wants kids eventually. That means marriage."

Amusement tinged CeeCee's words when she said, "If you barely know her, isn't it a bit premature to decide you don't want to marry her and father her children?"

"This isn't funny. I'm serious."

Her voice sobered. "I know you are. I just don't see the problem. Are you sure you're not making this more complicated than it needs to be?"

He let the silence hang. A flight attendant walked past and gave him a faint, distracted smile. When she was gone, he sighed and said, "I think Mom and Dad had it right. One marriage per person. Get it right the first time because you don't get another chance. Don't you remember those lectures?"

"That was a hyperbole and you know it," his

sister said. "They wanted to make sure we wouldn't go through three or four marriages like some people. They wanted us to be sure before we took our vows. And it worked, didn't it? I was positive I wanted to marry Jack. You were positive you wanted to marry Robyn." Now her voice softened. "Robyn's death was a terrible, awful thing. But it doesn't mean your entire marriage was a mistake."

"But what if it was?" he asked, and took a deep breath. "Some days I think that if she'd lived, we would've ended up divorced. We fought all the time. Hell, we fought the day she died."

And for that, he would never forgive himself.

"Couples fight," CeeCee said pragmatically. "Life goes on. Doesn't mean you would have divorced. And if you had, would the world truly have ended? You did your best. That's all anyone can ask."

"My best wasn't good enough." Seth flexed

his knee, which ached from his cramped position. "I don't want to go through that again." It wasn't worth the guilt, the shouts, the bad feelings.

"That's your choice." CeeCee sounded irritated now. "But don't you dare blame it on Mom and Dad for lectures they gave us when we were horny teenagers. They never meant you should stop living when Robyn died. Hell, call them if you don't believe me. They'll tell you themselves."

"No. That's okay." Seth closed his eyes, suddenly exhausted. "I hear you."

"You hear me but you don't believe me," CeeCee said. Her voice softened. "Give it a chance, Seth. Being lonely isn't going to bring Robyn back and it isn't going to change what happened—or didn't—between the two of you. It's time to start something new, find a different pattern."

"Maybe." But if that was the case, shouldn't he pick someone who was the opposite of his fractious wife? Shouldn't he look for a calm, stress-free relationship that would avoid the arguments, the accusations?

Hell, he didn't know anymore.

"Look, I've got to go," he said when the same flight attendant passed again, and this time tapped her watch to indicate that it was nearly time for the plane to take off. "I'll call you in a few days."

He ended the call more tangled up inside than ever.

When he returned to his seat and buckled in, Cassie shifted in her sleep and touched her head to his shoulder. She sighed softly and the faint wrinkle between her eyebrows faded.

Seth thought about easing her aside.

Instead, he laid his head back on the seat and closed his eyes while the plane taxied into position and accelerated, sending them home.

AS THEY DISEMBARKED from the plane, Cassie felt Seth's tension, but he brushed her off when she asked what was wrong. She snuck glances at him, and saw the angry set to his jaw and the coolness in his eyes. Beneath the annoyance, she thought she detected guilt. Reluctance. And that made her nervous.

She didn't press him for an explanation. Instead she ran through the Florida trip in her head, trying to figure out what had him so upset. It could be the case, of course, but she didn't think it was. His mood seemed too bleak for that. Too hurt.

So it was something she had done, or something she hadn't done. But what? What could she do to fix it? How could she—

Whoa. She stopped dead in the middle of the airport concourse, nearly causing a pedestrian pileup behind her.

Seth stopped and looked back. "Something wrong?"

Yes. Everything was wrong, she realized suddenly. She was doing it again. She was making excuses for the man in her life, trying to figure out what she had done to make him unhappy, what she could do to fix things.

Anger surged, not at him but at herself. At the weakness she thought she'd conquered when she left Lee.

Damn it, she knew better.

But that was her problem, not his, so she forced herself to walk. "No. Nothing's wrong."

They left the airport terminal, picked up Seth's truck from short-term parking and headed straight for the Bear Claw police station.

Annoyed with herself and the silence, Cassie punched Alissa's number into her cell. According to Alissa's last report, Denver Lyttle had admitted that he had driven Jasmine Gardner home from the slopes the afternoon before her murder, but said he'd dropped her off at home before six because she needed to get ready for a hot date.

With a solid alibi for the time of the murder—between ten that night and two the next morning—and an explanation of the witness testimony, Denver had been released.

Which sent them back nearly to square one. Suspicions but no suspects. Evidence but no concrete patterns.

Alissa's voice answered, sounding breathless and harried. She must have checked caller ID, because she immediately said, "Cassie, I need you to meet me at Hawthorne Hospital. Something's happened to Maya."

Cassie's heart jammed her throat. Oh, God. Not Maya. "What? What's wrong?"

Seth looked over at her tone, but she gestured for him to wait while she pressed the cell phone to her ear, willing the connection to stay strong as they passed under an overpass.

The connection fuzzed but held enough for her to hear Alissa say, "I'm not sure. Just get here!"

Cassie slapped the phone shut, pulse pounding. "We've got to go to the hospital. Maya's been hurt."

Without a word, Seth cut across three lanes of traffic, ignored the angry horn blasts and took the next exit, which dumped them in downtown Bear Claw, maybe five minutes from Hawthorne Memorial Hospital. "What happened?"

"I don't know." Cassie twisted her fingers together as a parade of images jammed her brain. Maya cheering and flushed with success when the three of them graduated from the academy. Maya playing the impromptu counselor, sitting Cassie down after another bad first date, prodding until the Lee situation had come spilling out. Maya telling her it wasn't her fault, urging her to take what she needed from the experience and move on.

Maya a few days ago, looking sad and lost and torn up over a child services case.

Guilt stabbed Cassie. She should've tried harder to find Maya, to make sure she was okay. The case was no excuse. Seth was no excuse. She should have been a better friend.

"We're here." Seth pulled his truck into the

Emergency dock and whistled. "And apparently, so is everyone else."

The ambulance bay was crammed with people. Satellite trucks were parked haphazardly in the visitors' area, and men and women with cameras and microphone booms jostled for position near the main E.R. doors. Smaller knots of people spread out to the edges, where brightly dressed on-camera talents did stand-up reports from the scene.

But the scene of what?

"Let me out here," Cassie ordered, reaching for the door.

"No way." Seth floored the gas and aimed for a semilegal parking space, sending a trio of media types scurrying out of the way. "This could be a distraction, a plan to get you unprotected."

"Seems pretty elaborate," Cassie argued, but stayed put until he'd parked and moved around to cover her back.

"At this point, I wouldn't put anything past

our guy. He's too smart. Likes the grand
gesture too much. So far it's been mostly small
stuff. My gut tells me he's planning something
big. There has to be *some* reason he wanted us
out of town for a few days. Maybe this was it."

But when they pushed their way through the
surging sea of reporters and found two be-
leaguered uniforms trying to clear the ambulance bays for actual emergencies, they
quickly learned that the frenzy had nothing to
do with the murders.

"Officer Cooper went after Wexton Henkes
with her sidearm," one of the uniforms told
Seth, pitching his voice low so the crowding reporters wouldn't hear. "Something happened
with his son and she snapped. Completely lost
it."

It took a moment for the words to register in
Cassie's brain, because they made no sense.
Supercool, supercontrolled Maya would never
do something like that. She just wouldn't.

Then the second half of the officer's report

penetrated. *Something happened with his son.* Cassie remembered Maya talking about the boy, Kiernan, remembered how she had taken the case so personally, how she had questioned the wisdom of sending him home to his family, even though there was no actual proof of abuse.

If something else had happened to the boy…

"Let me through." She pushed past the officers, aware of Seth at her heels. Under other circumstances she might have found his presence soothing, strengthening. But as she strode through the E.R. waiting room and headed for the main desk, his looming bulk itched along her nerve endings like an accusation.

She had been so focused on him, on trying to figure out what he wanted and how to get along with him, that she'd missed helping a friend.

"Cassie!" Alissa erupted from a nearby room. "Thank God you're here!" She barely spared a glance for Seth as she grabbed Cassie's arm and dragged her into the room.

Maya lay in a hospital bed, eyes closed, skin so pale it looked nearly translucent. Her chest rose and fell rhythmically.

Her wrists and ankles were bound with soft restraints.

"What happened?" Cassie asked tightly, afraid that if she let loose with all the questions at once she might explode. She wanted to reach for Seth's hand for support. At the same time, she wanted to ask him to leave. He wasn't part of this friendship.

Alissa touched Maya's lax foot. "I'm not entirely sure. From what I've been able to piece together, Kiernan Henkes was admitted earlier today with severe injuries." She pressed her lips together, then continued. "Maya heard about it and she…hell, she went nuts. I wasn't there, but I guess she drove out to Henkes's mansion, used her badge to get inside, and then just…lost it. Wexton Henkes says she was screaming at him and accusing him of all sorts of terrible things. She had a weapon, and I guess he grabbed for it, they struggled and the gun discharged. Henkes had a slice carved out of his arm. He says Maya slipped and fell during the struggle. Hit her head on the corner of a marble table. She's been out ever since, though the docs say she should've come around by now. They're wondering if there's something else going on."

Nausea twisted Cassie's stomach. Maya looked small in the hospital bed. Pale. Fragile. Cassie had never noticed before just how thin Maya's arms were, how narrow her wrist bones were. How had she never noticed that her friend was so delicate?

"Did the doctors have any suggestions?" Seth asked, his voice sounding too loud and masculine in the hushed hospital room.

Alissa glanced at him. "They think she took something—accidentally or on purpose—that altered her mental state and now has her unconscious. They're still waiting on the full tox screen. The alternative…" She paused, then said, "The alternative is that she's had some sort of mental breakdown. Her mind may be keeping her from waking up."

A chill skittered through Cassie. "That's ridiculous." But was it? Maya hadn't been herself over the past few days. She'd been stressed and unhappy ever since returning from the conference. Cassie had attributed it to the murders, but what if it had been something else entirely?

Something she would have seen if she'd been paying better attention.

"Good, you're all here" a new voice spoke from the doorway, startling all three of them. Chief Parry stood there, grim-faced. He glanced from Seth to Cassie and back. "You get anything useful from Fitz before the shooting?"

"A name," Seth answered. "Anna Susie. Mean any-thing to you?"

"Not a damn thing," the chief said bitterly.

"And it sure as hell isn't anything I can take to the media." He cursed. "We've got two bodies, we just released our only solid suspect, and now this." He gestured toward Maya's motionless body. But though his motions were brusque, his eyes mirrored his concern. "Henkes is outside right now, playing the wounded martyr, telling the camera that although his son's in critical condition and he has fifteen stitches in his arm, his heart goes out to Officer Cooper. That sort of thing." Parry grimaced. "The higher-ups want me to make a statement. You three got any ideas?"

Cassie had some ideas, all right, but she wasn't about to share them with the media, so she stayed silent. When the others did the same, the chief scowled, but didn't pursue the question. He gestured toward the door. "I need Varitek and someone from the forensics department at the task force meeting in a half hour. The other tech stays with her. I want her guarded until we have a better handle on what happened."

"I'll stay," Alissa volunteered. She nodded to Cassie and Seth. "You two should be at the meeting."

Cassie had to force herself out of the room, had to force herself not to look back at Maya. Nerves twisted in her stomach. What had happened? It didn't seem to have anything to do with the murders, but still...

The timing seemed too coincidental.

She and Seth backtracked through the E.R. and out into the waiting room, but stopped just inside the doors at the sight of the mob outside. "Maybe we should go out another way."

"Good idea." Seth gestured for Cassie to lead.

As Cassie led Seth to a side exit, she couldn't get Maya out of her mind. The psych specialist had looked so fragile. So breakable. So she said, "Once we've got this case closed, I hope you'll be able to stick around for a few days. I could probably use your help with Henkes."

Seth paused on the stairs and turned to her.

Standing two steps below her, he was just shy of her height, so she had the strange sensation of looking down at him. The serious intensity of his eyes brought her up short and sent a chill skittering through her gut.

"I won't be staying after the case is closed." His expression was guarded, his voice laced with a thread of regret.

Cassie felt like she'd been gut-punched, not by his seemingly harmless words, but by the sudden suspicion that entered her soul. "What are you saying?"

The strong muscles of his throat moved as he swallowed. "I'm just making sure we understand each other. Things got…intense last night. I don't want either of us to make more of it than we should."

"You mean you don't want *me* to make more of it," she countered, feeling an icy wash of embarrassment and clutching disappointment spread through her body. "Wow. That's insulting. Just because I'm a woman, you assume

I'm going to equate good sex with love, is that it?" Her voice sharpened because maybe some small part of her had begun to think past tomorrow, had begun to wonder whether they might have a future.

"No, that's not it." But the protest lacked force. "I'm just trying to be fair here." He lifted his hands to her hips and held her in place as though he had the right to touch her. "Look, this could get out of hand if we let it."

A fluttering, panicked feeling pressed in Cassie's chest. She knew this wasn't the time or the place for this conversation, but couldn't bring herself to end it, couldn't force herself to step away from his hands and agree that yes, he was right. Instead, she gripped his wrists where they braced her. "And why would that be a bad thing? Explain it to me, because I'm sure as hell confused right now." She continued before he could answer, as the feelings built up inside her and spilled over in a torrent of words. "We like each other. We're good in bed together. Hell, we're even in the same field, so there isn't any problem with the hours or the expectations. Why not give it a try? We might surprise you."

The word *we* shimmered in the air between them like a promise. A plea.

But he shook his head. "I don't want what you want."

"Which is?"

"Kids. Family. Marriage. Any of it." When she didn't answer right away, he sighed heavily. "Look, I was the best husband I knew how to be, and it didn't sit easy with me. I wasn't good at compromise."

"You still aren't," Cassie countered, "and for some reason that doesn't bother me." She took a deep breath, trying to react with logic rather than emotion. She felt as though they were teetering atop a precipice, ready to slide down one side or the other, and her next words could tip the balance. "Look, I'll admit that little Eden has me thinking I'll want a baby eventually, but that's the key. Eventually. I'm not looking for a husband right now and I'm not looking to start a family right now. Why not give us a try for a while?"

He cocked his head. "You'd do that, even knowing nothing would ever come of it?"

"Sure," she said, thinking she could change his mind over time, or adjust her needs to suit his. "We're both grown-ups, we can compromise on—"

She stopped suddenly, hearing herself from a distance, as though she'd stepped outside her own skull for a moment.

What was she doing? This wasn't a compromise. This was her agreeing to a no-strings, no-future relationship when she knew damn well she wanted a husband and a family.

"Never mind," she said slowly. "You're right. That's not what I want and I'm not giving in this time."

He nodded, eyes dark. "You deserve someone who can give you the world."

"I don't want the world, I want you." She stared at him, anger stirring in her stomach. "But you're not willing to take that risk, are you? You're afraid you might make another mistake, and then where would you be?"

He scowled. "I'm more worried about you. I don't want to hurt another woman I—" He stalled before saying the word. "Another woman I care about."

"No," she countered, "you're afraid of hurting yourself." Disappointment and the screaming, howling unfairness of it roared through her. She wanted to shout at him for being craven, to beg him to give her a chance. But rather than say anything more, she leaned forward on the stairs, leaned into the hands that still gripped her hips as though she were his lifeline—

And she kissed him.

She felt him stiffen in shock. His forearms flexed beneath her hands and his fingers dug into her hips for an instant before he muttered something deep and dark, and opened his lips beneath hers.

She tightened her grip and leaned into him, poured herself into the kiss, trying to imprint herself on his soul. The heat rose between them, tangled with the wild ache for sex. For completion. The need was sharper now, made more intense by the fact that she knew what he tasted like, what he felt like surrounding her. Inside her.

It was that very knowledge that gave her the strength to pull away from him, even as her heart split in two. Damn him for doing this now.

Damn him for doing it at all.

She stared down at him while both their lungs worked, both their hearts pounded in the rhythm of sex. Of love.

He pressed his lips together, but left his hands hanging at his sides, as though he lacked the strength to shove them into his pockets. "What was that for?"

"So you'll remember what you're missing. You win. It's over." She tossed her hair and hoped she looked mad rather than desperate when she said, "But if you ever decide you want another chance, make sure you leave your dead wife out of it. I'm tired of having three-way conversations with her sitting smack in the middle. You come to me alone or don't come at all."

She pushed past him on the stairs and forced herself not to lift her fingertips to her lips, which felt warm and swollen. Instead, she lifted her chin and stalked toward the exit.

She slammed the door behind her.

And tried to will the tears away.

Chapter Thirteen

Cassie's words echoed in the strained silence as Seth drove them both to the police department. *A three-way conversation.*

Why had that struck a chord?

It wasn't just because she had a point—he knew he'd let Robyn's memory hover near them on more than one occasion. It was something else.

Something about the case.

He cursed under his breath as he pulled into the back parking lot of the Bear Claw Police Department. He was aware of Cassie's stony, hurt silence and his own mixed emotions. Regardless of CeeCee's opinions on marriage and second chances, he knew he'd done the right thing to nip his and Cassie's affair in the bud before emotions were involved.

That logic rang false as he jumped down out of the truck and felt a hollow ache within, but he pushed it aside and focused on the case, trying to ignore the tense set of Cassie's shoulders and his own desire to pull her close and apologize until her lips softened and she kissed him again.

Which would only put them back at square one.

A three-way conversation. The words played at the edges of his mind, alongside Fitz's scrawl. *Anna Susie.* He almost had it. The connections almost made sense in his brain.

But not quite.

They walked into the conference room, where Chief Parry was already at the podium. With his tie done up tight to his throat—a remnant of his televised briefing, no doubt—he looked uncomfortable. Angry. There was a stir in the room when Cassie entered, a buzz of whispers.

Until that moment, Seth hadn't thought

about what Maya's outburst would mean to the forensics department.

"Good. You're just in time." The chief stepped aside. "I'd like you two to walk us through what happened in Florida and how it fits into the case."

"I'll let Varitek handle it," Cassie said quietly. She avoided the glares and took her habitual seat at the edge of the room. Without Alissa or Maya nearby, she sat alone.

Seth glanced at her and took a half step in her direction before deciding to leave well enough alone. But his heart was heavy as he made his way to the podium and brought the others up to speed on the events in Florida, and the results his team had come up with while he and Cassie had been on the road.

There were a few new pieces of data. Seth's crew had processed two DNA samples. The first was from the red hat and dark jacket Cassie's attacker had dropped after sabotaging her brakes. The second was from the skin tag of a single short hair—maybe an arm hair?—they had found wedged beneath one of Peter Dunbar's fingernails. They were a match. Final confirmation that Cassie had been targeted by the killer.

After the DNA evidence, Seth gave the others a brief rundown on the evidence that remained to be processed, but it was precious little. They needed something more. They needed a break. But as Seth sat down and the meeting progressed, it became obvious that the other cops were suffering from the same limitations.

Not enough evidence. Or rather, too much evidence, not all of which fit into a clear, coherent pattern.

Finally, Chief Parry retook the podium. He'd pulled his tie off and jammed it in his breast pocket, but his face remained grim. "Before we break, I'd like to make sure we're all on the same page regarding the Henkes matter." He scanned the room, eyes lighting on a number of the more outspoken task force members. "If anyone asks you about Wexton Henkes, his son Kiernan, Officer Cooper, or any related matter, you are to say 'no comment.' Period. Until we know what went down today, I want your lips zipped, understand?"

Most of the task force members nodded or murmured agreement. Others were not so kind.

Piedmont spoke up first. "No comment is fine for the reporters, but how about us? What about our right to know?" He stood and glanced around him, and received a few nods, a few uncomfortable smiles. "And what does this mean for the forensics department?" He gestured toward Cassie without looking at her. "Unless it's escaped your attention, the FBI's been doing all of our forensics lately. Why spend money on these three? Why not just outsource?"

"Piedmont, that's enough." The chief's voice was deadly even. "Sit down." When the homicide detective had obeyed his chief's order, Parry glared around the room. "Anyone else have any other bright ideas along those lines? No? Good, then let's—"

"Chief?" Cassie's voice broke in. Seth jerked his head in her direction. Her shoulders were set and her eyes crackled with the sort of prickly anger he hadn't seen much of in the past few days. Not since she'd walked into that drab studio apartment and seen him hunched over her crime scene. She stood, fists clenched, every line of her body screaming that she was ready to do battle. "I'd like to say something. I think it's time we cleared up a few misconceptions about the crime lab."

Oh hell, Seth thought. *This is going to be ugly.*

WHEN PARRY GESTURED for her to go ahead, Cassie's heart pounded into her throat, but she knew she had to do this. The others weren't there to defend themselves. It was up to her.

She stood in the corner, not taking the

podium, but rather turning toward the back of the room, where the other cops sat in knots, vaguely grouped by rank or specialty.

When she spoke, she focused on Piedmont and his partner, Mendoza. They had been the most vocal in their opposition to the Forensics Department from day one.

"You don't have to like us personally," she began, aware of Seth sitting off to one side, watching her with cool green eyes that hid what he was thinking. "I can't tell you who to like or how to act any more than the chief can. But—" she emphasized the word with a pause "—I can tell you to look at the evidence." She scanned the room, skipped over Seth, and returned her attention to Piedmont before she continued. "Since Maya, Alissa and I took over Bear Claw forensics, your evidence turn-around rates are up, your case clearance rates are up, and you've had fewer cases thrown out on evidentiary problems. I know. I checked."

Piedmont scowled. "So what? We're paying for three of you to do one man's job. We should be seeing a three-hundred percent improvement. Instead, one of you is playing slap-and-tickle with Tucker McDermott, one is in the hospital halfway to a section eight, and you're—"

"I'm here, and I'm doing my job," Cassie interrupted, "which is more than I can say for you at the moment. You seem more interested in causing a fuss than solving crime."

She was aware that maybe half of the cops in the room looked uncomfortable, like they wished Piedmont would just shut up. She wasn't sure what she'd ever done to the surly homicide detective, and she was pretty sure she couldn't fix it now. But amazingly…his words hadn't crushed her. They hadn't demolished her. They hadn't proved that she couldn't cut it, couldn't hack it, couldn't do the job.

She pressed her lips together for a moment, listening for Lee's voice in her mind.

It was silent.

Wow. She'd finally banished his ghost, and all it had taken was standing up to Bear Claw's schoolyard bully. She almost smiled, but didn't, because her revelation didn't change a damn thing. The other cops still hated her, they still had a murderer to catch, Maya was still in the hospital, and Seth was still…

Well, he was still Seth. Unattainable. Unapproachable.

Damn him.

So she fisted her hands at her sides, aware of the speculative looks from her supposed coworkers, and said, "Maya Cooper is a good cop. Stick with 'no comment' or you'll answer to me. Now, if that's all, I'll be in the damn basement. Don't bother me."

She turned and stalked from the room, partly to make an exit and partly because she couldn't stand to be in there anymore. The walls were too close, the air too close, as though even in a room with thirty-some cops, it was only her and Seth.

Damn him. Was he a coward for not trying again, or was she just not good enough to make him want to bother?

Never mind, she told her internal voice, *don't answer that.*

She didn't want to know.

The desk officer raised an eyebrow when she blew past the front desk. "Task force meeting done?"

"No, but I have work to do."

Temper carried her downstairs and through the lab, but instead of powering up the machines, she sank into her desk chair and felt a heavy beat of depression at the emptiness of the space around her. She wished Alissa were there to tell her she'd done an okay job of keeping it civil upstairs. She wished Maya were there to tell her she'd been right to end things with Seth. She wished—

The four-line phone on her desk rang. The fourth light blinked red, indicating that the call was coming in on her direct line. The caller ID showed that the number was blocked, even from the police system, which should have been impossible.

A chill shimmied through Cassie's body. Nobody had the direct number except Maya and Alissa, and she was pretty sure the hospital should show up on caller ID.

Shouldn't it?

It could be a prank, she told herself. A hoax. A sales call. But her fingers trembled ever so slightly when she grabbed the handset.

"Bear Claw crime lab," she answered professionally, half expecting the click of a disconnect.

Instead, she got a voice. Low, distorted, like the man on the other end of the line feared he would be overheard. "There's a present waiting for you on the back step. Go get it and come back to this phone without speaking to anyone or signaling anyone. You have thirty seconds."

Cassie's heart jammed her throat, then raced into overdrive. Her palms dampened and adrenaline sizzled through her body. "Wait!" she said quickly. "What sort of present? I'm not picking up anything that—"

"You have twenty-five seconds," the voice interrupted. "If you don't follow instructions, she's dead." There was a shift of movement, then a female scream, high and terrified.

Christ! Cassie didn't stop to ask who or why. She was out of the office at a run moments later, gunning for the back door. She didn't know who had screamed, but she absolutely, positively believed that the speaker would kill without mercy.

He already had.

To hell with not signaling anyone. She waved frantically at the hallway cameras and pantomimed a phone call, hoping the desk officer was watching, hoping he'd get the hint.

The seconds ticked away in her brain. She slammed open the back door, then threw herself to the side, half expecting that the promised "present" would be a hail of gunfire.

But there was no sound, no bullets. Just a small cardboard jewelry box sitting on the steps.

These days, an explosive the size of a pencil tip can wipe out an entire building, she remembered Sawyer saying. But though the bomb expert knew his stuff, she didn't have time for subtlety.

She grabbed the box and ran. When she reached her office, she snatched up the phone. "I've got it. Hello? I've got it."

But her exertion-sped breaths echoed into a silent receiver. Damn! Was she too late?

Not willing to accept that option, she yanked open her desk drawer and pulled out a set of gloves and a pair of tweezers. She'd already messed with the outside of the box, but there was no need to sully the evidence on the inside. Working quickly but carefully, she eased the lid off the box to reveal a square of cotton batting. She used the tweezers to pull the batting up, and gasped.

"Oh, God." She swallowed hard and ordered her stomach to stay put. It was a fingertip.

A fresh one.

"Officer Dumont?"

It took her a crazed moment to realize the voice was coming from the receiver she'd dropped on the desk, not from the finger, which glistened red with blood, pink with chipped, feminine nail polish and gray with the pallor of death.

Neither Alissa nor Maya would be caught dead in pink polish, and the other female officers were upstairs. So this was someone else, an innocent caught up in the killer's evil game.

Cassie snatched up the phone. "Where is she? What have you done to her? What do you want?"

The answering chuckle was dry, and gave nothing away. "To answer your questions in order, I have her with me, she's fine except for the regrettable loss of a digit, and I want you."

The last three words were delivered in a low, silky tone. *I want you.* She'd heard the same thing from Seth—was it only the night before? It seemed like forever. But the intent had been so different. Then, she had shivered with excitement.

Now, she shivered with dread. But she was a cop, and she was tough enough for the badge and the job. So she stiffened her spine and said, "Where."

She didn't even make the single word sound like a question.

"Walk out the back door. Don't speak to anyone, and don't try waving at the cameras again. I'll see you but they won't."

A shiver worked its way through her when she realized he'd somehow preempted the P.D. cameras. That was how he'd managed to sneak in undetected. He wasn't a cop at all.

Or maybe he was. She didn't know anymore.

She licked her suddenly dry lips. "And then?"

"Leave your cell phone and your weapon on the desk. I'll be watching, so don't mess with me. There's a blue hatchback in the parking lot, next to the exit. The keys are tucked in the visor and there's a cell phone in the glove box. Start driving. You'll get your orders once you're on the road. You have sixty seconds." There was a pause. Harsh breathing. Then his final words, delivered in such a menacing tone that she couldn't help believing him when he said, "Any wrong moves and I'll kill her. It'd be a shame, too. She's such a pretty thing."

And the line went dead.

Cassie was out the door in a heartbeat, then skidded to a stop and reversed direction. She yanked open the lab freezer, grabbed a scoop of crushed ice and plonked the fingertip in the middle. Then she left the mess on her desk along with a hastily scrawled note.

And ran.

Chapter Fourteen

Seth wanted to go after Cassie when she fled, but he didn't dare. It would cause too much talk. And besides, he didn't have the right to comfort her.

Not anymore.

So instead of following her, he stood and retook the podium without waiting for the chief's go-ahead. He glared at Piedmont. "I won't beleaguer the point Officer Dumont has already made except to say that I consider her a top-notch evidence technician, and I would be proud to work with her again."

As he stepped away from the podium, he realized it was the absolute truth, which was almost a surprise. When they had first teamed up, he'd been unable to see past the legs and that long, blond hair. When had she gone from being a woman to a cop in his brain?

She hadn't, he realized. She was both of those things.

He retook his seat as the chief closed the meeting by shifting a few assignments and repeating that they were to have "no comment" about the Henkes incident. Seth listened with half his attention while he thought about his revelation.

Cassie was an attractive woman and a cop, and she was damn good at being both. Two halves of a whole. Two sides of a single coin.

He glanced up behind the chief at the case board, which held pictures and notes from the Canyon kidnappings on one side, the newer pictures and data on the other side. The end result looked schizophrenic, like they were trying to make a whole out of two unrelated halves.

The words echoed in his head. Two halves of a whole. Two sides of a single coin.

And then Seth saw it. *No,* he thought as the meeting finally dispersed and his vision was obscured for a moment by a press of bodies heading for the exit. *Not two. Three. A three-way conversation.*

Three men. The kidnapper, Bradford Croft. Their murderer…and someone else. A mastermind who had brought two completely different criminals together for a common goal.

To destabilize the Bear Claw P.D.

The room cleared as the theory took shape in his head. He wasn't sure that it would help them find their man, but it explained too many inconsistencies to be a figment.

"Something wrong?" the chief asked, pausing beside Seth's chair.

"Yes." Then Seth shook his head. "No, nothing's wrong. I'm thinking…I think—"

A female scream split the air, muffled by distance and walls, jolting him to his feet in an instant. He bolted for the lobby with the chief on his heels, instinctively knowing where the scream had come from.

The basement.

Cassie's lab.

His heart pounded in his chest, nearly bursting through his rib cage as he hurdled the stairs in two strides and charged into the forensics department.

Alissa stood near Cassie's desk, hands pressed to her mouth, eyes wide and dark. She turned to him the moment he entered. "Tucker said he'd…stay with Maya. I came to talk to Cassie and found…" she swallowed, got herself under control and said, "I found this."

"What is it?" He strode to her side. "Where's Cassie?"

But he didn't need her to tell him Cassie was gone.

Not when he saw the bucket of melting ice and a single fingertip.

His stomach took a quick trip to his toes and leapt up into his throat on a shout that he jammed behind his clenched teeth. He reached toward the fingertip, and training barely overrode the overwhelming desire to snatch it up.

"Polish." He forced the word between his teeth. "Cassie wears pink polish."

"Not the same shade," Alissa said quickly, but she didn't sound sure. She pointed to a single sheet of paper lying on the desk. "And she left us a note. She wouldn't have done that if…" She trailed off.

Aware of the other cops arriving at his back, staring over his shoulders or milling in the doorway, Varitek leaned forward and read a pair of sentences hurriedly scrawled on the paper.

Blue hatchback in the parking lot. I'm counting on you to back me up.

DRIVING WITH BOTH HANDS on the wheel and the cheap single-use cell phone clamped between her ear and shoulder, Cassie ran every red light she could and swerved into oncoming traffic at regular intervals.

Come on, she thought with all her mental might. *Come on! Where's a cop when you want to get pulled over?*

But she didn't say it aloud because the cell connection was live. She couldn't hear anything at the other end, but that didn't mean he wasn't listening. He might not be able to see her anymore by camera, and she was pretty sure he wasn't tailing her as she followed his obscure, circuitous directions through the city, but she'd bet money that there was a GPS tracker somewhere in the vehicle or the phone. He'd know if she turned off the planned route.

Whoever *he* was.

She'd passed through fear and hit determination. The fine tremor in her fingers was adrenaline, not nerves, and the sick feeling was anxiety for the woman hostage, not herself.

At least that was what she told herself. But deep down inside, she knew there was fear, as well. She was cut off from her backup. Alone.

"Take your next right," the voice said suddenly against her ear, making her jolt and swerve unintentionally.

She made the turn without comment, having already found that he wouldn't answer questions, wouldn't respond to a damn thing she said. It almost made her wonder whether the receiver was muted at her end.

Could she use that somehow?

Could she trust it enough to dare?

Where are you, Seth? she wondered, knowing that she'd gone from wanting to see any cop to seeing him, specifically. He should have found the iced fingertip by now, should have seen the note. Depending on the status of the parking lot cameras, they should be looking for her even now, because at least the voice hadn't forced her to dump the—

"Pull in here," he said. "Park beside the white sedan with the ragtop."

She cursed under her breath and did as she was told, but she knew what would come next.

Hell, it was what she would do, and the voice on the other end of the phone had already proved he was equally as clever as the Bear Claw P.D.

She only hoped he wasn't as clever as a single FBI agent.

Seth would come after her. He wouldn't stop until he'd found her.

Right?

The fact that she wasn't entirely certain brought a shiver. What if nobody had headed down into the lab yet to see if she was okay? What if they didn't even know she was gone?

The loneliness closed in, nearly suffocating her, making her wonder whether it was truly better to be alone than to be in a relationship with someone she loved, compromises or not.

"Leave the phone and get in the white car. The keys are under the floor mat on the driver's side. You'll find a map under the seat. Follow it. You have five minutes or she's dead."

The line clicked off.

"Damn it," she said, finally able to speak aloud. "Damn you!"

But she hustled out of the hatchback, leaving the door open and the phone on the seat. What could she leave as evidence, as a clue that she'd been there, that she was going somewhere else?

That damn clock ticked down in her head. He'd said five minutes. She had maybe four and a half left.

She grabbed the map, took a quick look at it—

And had an idea.

SETH DROVE at the edge of safety, weaving through the city, looking for the blue hatchback they'd just been able to glimpse a corner of on the parking lot cameras. They'd gotten three numbers off the plate, but that would be enough.

It *had* to be enough.

The radio crackled to life at his elbow. "Blue hatchback alpha-bravo-bravo-three-niner-one-one has been spotted in a short-term parking lot on Post Office Road." The dispatcher went on to order units to the area, but Seth was already on it. His truck didn't have lights or a siren, but the other drivers got out of his way when he hit the gas and the horn, and raced toward the address.

They had reported finding the car, but not the cop.

Not Cassie.

He battled mental images of Robyn. But for the first time in what seemed like forever, they were secondary memories, crowded out by newer, fresher mental pictures. Cassie looking up at him from a soft nest of pillows and body-warmed sheets. Cassie getting in his face, eyes sparking with temper, with passion.

She had so much passion inside her.

God, he thought, she'd better be okay. If she wasn't—

It didn't even bear thinking about. She was okay. She'd be okay.

The words spooled in his brain like a mantra

as he careened into the short-term parking lot on two wheels, right behind the first BCCPD unit on scene. He slammed the truck into Park and leapt from the cab. "Stay back! Nobody tromps on my evidence!"

Not at what was easily the most important crime scene he'd ever worked, personally, if not professionally.

The thought barely even gave him pause. Yeah, it was personal for him now. Had been for longer than he wanted to admit. He didn't know what he was going to do about it, where he wanted it to go, but he damn sure knew he and Cassie were going to have to rewind that last talk once he found her.

If he found her.

No. He wouldn't think that way. He *would* find her, he *would* talk to her, and this time he wouldn't be a coward. He'd find a way they could make it work. He'd change or she would. Hell, they both would. Whatever it took. He'd marry her. Give her children. Hell, he'd have her children if that was what it took to—

With those emotionally charged, disorganized thoughts rocketing around in his brain, Seth approached the blue hatchback. The driver's side door was open, nearly touching the car beside it, a black SUV with its engine still ticking as it cooled down.

The SUV had been parked recently, he thought, as though a space had opened up.

"There's a cell phone on the driver's seat," one of the cops said. He was a younger uniform Seth hadn't dealt with before, but he and his partner stood solidly aside, following orders not to mess up the scene.

Liking the younger cops' fidget-free calm, Seth nodded toward the road. "Tell the others to park on the street. I don't want anyone else in this lot until we've processed the scene. I think she took another car from here."

That had to have been how it played out. There was no blood, no signs of a struggle in the slushy fringe at the edge of the lot, no evidence that she'd been hurt.

Please, God, don't let her be hurt.

With anger and worry a hard, hot ball in his gut, Seth stepped to the front of the car and looked down at the single-use cell phone sitting in the front seat. He examined the evidence without touching, knowing it was very possible that they'd need all the trace they could get. The killer or his master had planted the car in the P.D. parking lot.

Seth tried to clear his mind for the job, tried to empty himself of everything but the evidence.

He failed. There was too much worry clogging him, too much emotion. When was the last time he'd felt this much emotion, this much anger and fear?

Robyn, he thought automatically, then corrected himself. No, this was worse. Robyn's attack had happened so quickly, so unexpectedly. He hadn't had time to process the horror before it was over.

But this situation…he was chasing a lukewarm trail. Worse, he knew without a doubt that Cassie had gone willingly, called by duty, by ambition.

By the fact that she was a damn good cop.

When he'd first met her, he'd thought he couldn't handle being with someone who flung herself into danger with the same abandon he used in his work. Now he knew better. Cassie wouldn't be Cassie without that go-to-hell attitude and fearlessness. She wouldn't be the woman who'd first attracted him, who'd broken through the barriers he'd erected after Robyn's death.

Without her thirst for solitary danger, she wouldn't be the woman he'd fallen in love with.

The word *love* sliced through him like a velvet-edged sword, too little, too late. Or was it?

"Not on my watch," he said aloud, and bent toward the cell phone. As he did so, a spear of sunlight broke through the cloud cover and glinted off the side of the hatchback.

At the cryptic message written on the dusty paint of the rear quarter panel in a cramped scrawl.

Anasazi.

Oh hell, Seth thought as the fine hairs on his nape prickled. They'd had it for days. Not Anna Susie. Anasazi. The name of the Native American group being featured in the new exhibit at the Natural History Museum. But why?

Why would the mastermind give them a name?

Because, Seth realized as he bolted for his truck, he wanted them to find Cassie, just as the Diablo brothers had wanted him to find Robyn. Only this time, Seth vowed, he'd damn well be in time to keep the woman he loved from taking her last breath.

Or he'd die trying.

"ANNA SUSIE," Cassie said to herself as she climbed the stairs to the Bear Claw Natural

History Museum, which was closed while they built the much-lauded new exhibit. "Anasazi. I get it, but why?"

As the quick spring dusk fell over Bear Claw, she tried the door and found it unlocked.

Her enemy knew someone within the museum, or else he worked there in his "real" life. She filed the observation, but had a feeling she wouldn't need it. The case would be closed for her tonight.

One way or the other.

Her footfalls echoed strangely in the deserted lobby, making alone feel all that much more lonely. She had an almost over-whelming urge to turn tail and run, to pick up the phone in the ticket booth and call for help, to do something, anything but walk deeper into the too-quiet museum.

But she forged onward with the image of a bloody fingertip held firmly at the forefront of her brain. The hostage was a victim. An innocent of Bear Claw. One of Cassie's own.

She was a Bear Claw cop now. They were her responsibility. Her people.

The thought made her feel less alone. Unfortunately, so did the sudden creeping sensation of being watched.

Of being hunted.

The note in the white ragtop had said only to go to the museum. Now, as she passed the gift shop and neared a half-finished composite archway, she wondered whether this was such a good idea. But what other choice did she have? She would have to keep going and trust that Seth would get her back.

The archway had been sculpted to look like rock, like the entrance to a cave. The air was cool and damp, though she wasn't sure whether that was a special effect or a by-product of the moist spring chill.

You have five minutes, the voice had said, but was that five minutes to reach the museum or five minutes to find the next clue? If the latter, she was dangerously close to running out of time. Knowing it, knowing she'd come this far and damn well wasn't going to back down now, she steeled herself and stepped through the arch, into the mostly completed Anasazi exhibit.

The archway led to a tunnel, with a rock-painted roof that hung low overhead and walls that pressed in on her, bringing her back in time. There were petroglyphs carved and marked on the cave walls, symbols she recognized from books and hiking trips, an amalgam of Anasazi and other cultures no doubt intended to set the mood of ancient times and other worlds without relying too heavily on accuracy.

"It's working," Cassie whispered to herself, needing the human sound as she worked her way through the tunnel. The atmosphere clung to her, making her feel as though her humanity, her civilization was being stripped away layer by layer.

When she reached the end of the tunnel, she swore she heard a slide of footstep behind her.

She spun, slapped for the weapon that was no longer at the small of her back, and called, "Who's there?" When there was no answer, no more motion, the fine hairs on the back of her neck rippled, and she shouted, "Show yourself, you coward! Step out here now, or I'm coming after you!"

An amplified voice chuckled in response, bouncing from speakers that must be hidden amongst the stones, which seemed more and more real by the moment. "There's no need to shout, Officer Dumont, and no need to threaten. We're waiting for you. Just keep walking."

She stood where she was. "I want an assurance that you'll let the hostage go. You want me, right? Well, you've got me. Just let her go!"

She expected a mocking laugh. She wasn't disappointed.

"Now where is the fun in that?" the voice asked on a chuckle. Only now she realized it wasn't the same voice as on the phone. Even through the fuzz of mechanical distortion, this voice was deeper, darker.

There was another man.

She lifted her chin, not knowing whether he could see, but needing the defiant gesture for herself. "I'm not here for fun. I'm here to arrest both of you."

"Stop stalling." The voice cracked angrily from the loudspeakers. "You have ten seconds to reach the chamber."

A woman's scream sounded up ahead, spurring Cassie onward. Mental clock ticking down the seconds, she ran until she burst out of the tunnel and into a central courtyard of stone.

Signs pointed out the various exhibits. A splash of dark red wetness marked one, and Cassie followed the arrow beneath at a run, hoping the blood was from the woman's finger wound and not something more serious.

Something more fatal.

The offshoot tunnel was a warmer tan color,

sandy instead of dark rock, and marked with flowing, spiritual pictograms. She paid them little heed as, lungs heaving, she skidded into the chamber.

The exhibit was meant to be a kiva, a beehive-shaped room of the type the Anasazi had used for spiritual reflection and religious practices.

But the shrine had been perverted by a madman.

Redness splashed the walls, dripped down and pooled on the floor. The lax body of a woman lay off to one side. He hadn't even bothered to pose her. He'd just dropped her when her arterial spurts had faded in death. A pair of surgical gloves lay nearby, along with a flipped-open five-inch buck knife that was covered in blood.

Cassie's stomach dropped and her heart clogged her mouth. She was too damn late. The woman's skin hadn't gone gray-blue with death yet, but the smell of it was in the air. The finality of it coated the inside of Cassie's mouth and sinuses, and crept cold fingers into her heart.

Knowing it, hating him for it, she focused her attention on the lone man standing in the center of the domed room. He was in his late thirties, and of medium height and build, though the way he stood hinted at muscle and strength beneath the loose pullover and crisp new blue jeans. His brown hair was neatly trimmed and his brown leather shoes matched his belt. He looked like a businessman on casual Friday, come to the museum for lunch.

Until she stared into his eyes. They were winter-cold, an ice-blue that showed no hint of expression. They simply held…nothing as they looked at her, looked through her as though the man wasn't even sure why she was there.

Fear, pure and icy, washed through Cassie as she finally understood what she'd gotten herself into. She had no weapon, no plan, and her backup was more hope than reality.

What the hell had she been thinking?

She hadn't been thinking, she realized. She'd been reacting to the threat, to the victim.

Now the victim was gone. The killer had no more hold on her.

Cassie took a step back. Then another. The man's eyes didn't shift. He didn't speak, didn't react, as though he was made of wax, or maybe the composite that had been used to form the mud daub of the fake Anasazi temple.

Heart slamming in her ribs, Cassie turned to flee, to escape the smell of blood and the sight of death.

A rock-painted panel slid into place, trapping her in the kiva with the dead-eyed man. A loud, satisfied chuckle sounded from the loudspeakers. "Not yet, Officer Dumont. The fun's barely even started!" There was a pause, then the voice said, "Nevada? Will you please restrain Officer Dumont while we wait for the others?"

Nevada. The name rang a faint bell. That had been the name of the drifter who'd briefly lived in the first crime scene apartment. She didn't know anything else about him, but wondered whether it was a coincidence that their other suspect had been named after a place. Denver. Nevada. Any connection?

Then it was past time to wonder. The dead-eyed man came at her in a rush.

Cassie lashed out a kick and shifted on the balls of her feet when he closed in. Heart pounding, mind racing, she worked her way around, turning him toward the body, so she could slide a step closer to the bloody knife. Another step. Almost there.

"My name is Cassie. Did you know that? And your name's Nevada, right?" She talked, hoping to distract him, to hide her intentions from the voice on the loudspeaker. She didn't know whether the other man could see into the kiva itself, whether he had control of the museum cameras or not.

"You don't need to do this, Nevada." She shifted sideways, wanting to duck down and grab the knife, but sure her adversary would lunge the moment she did. "You don't have to listen to him. We can help you."

Something flickered in those chill eyes.

She pressed the advantage. "We can help you. We know you didn't mean any of it."

Those cold blue eyes flickered again, but this time with mirth. Nevada's lips curved. "Oh, but I did mean to do it, Officer Dumont. And I enjoyed it. The slut taught me well." He licked his lips and closed in on her, crowding her against the textured kiva wall.

Heart pounding, Cassie broke to the side, knowing that the fire code would require a second exit from the kiva but not having a clue where they'd stashed it. She ran from Nevada, but he only laughed and followed at a leisurely pace.

"It's a round room," he called. "You're not going anywhere."

"Excellent!" the disembodied voice said over the loudspeakers. "Her friends are here, with the FBI agent in the lead. Sorry there's no viewscreen. You'll have to take my word for it."

Cassie froze at the words *FBI agent.* Seth! He'd come for her!

Nevada grabbed her in that instant, and yanked her arm up behind her back. She screeched and fought, and shouted "Seth!" as loud as she could, not knowing if her voice would penetrate the intricate maze of tunnels and composite. "Seth, I'm in the kiva!"

"That did it," the voice said, satisfied. "He's headed this way now. Too bad for him he's already dead."

There was a click.

The rapid beep of a digital countdown.

And a searing, howling explosion.

Chapter Fifteen

Seth heard her voice, and bolted toward the sound, toward his woman, not caring that he left the other Bear Claw cops behind.

Forget backup. This was personal.

He lunged through a fake stone archway, his only concern getting to her before it was too late. He charged down a tunnel that was so narrow he had to duck down inside it, and cursed under his breath as he ran.

She'd better be okay, he kept thinking, or the bastard was dead. No due process, no Miranda, nothing.

Just dead.

He saw a light at the end of the tunnel and

hurtled toward it, knowing she had to be near, knowing he just had to—

An explosion ripped through the tunnel, through the very fabric of the building, as though the world was ending with him in the middle of the chaos.

The shock wave blasted Seth off his feet and sent him sprawling into a larger space, where signs and corridors radiated off from a pseudo-archaeological site. He hit hard and cursed a punch of pain, but kept rolling until he slammed up against a wall. He struggled to his knees, pulled his weapon and fanned the area.

Deserted.

The tunnel he'd come from was completely demolished. He could hear shouts and groans from the other side, and knew some of the others had been trapped. Dust and fumes and chunks of rubble belched from the tunnel, warning him there would be no backup.

He was on his own.

He tried not to think about the men who

were trapped beneath the collapsed tunnel. It hadn't been made of stone, but the composite had been laid over steel supports and heavy sheets of plywood. That was bad enough.

Then the sprinkler system cut in with a thump and a hiss, and water rained down on him.

Seth cursed and hauled himself to his feet. His only hope was that the bomber would assume he'd been caught in the tunnel blast. That might give him an edge. An opportunity to get to Cassie.

With her image fixed in his mind, all attitude and hidden vulnerability, he struggled to his feet, weapon in his hand. He didn't need to look far for evidence. A red smear mocked him from an arrowed sign.

He tried not to wonder whether it was her blood or another's, tried not to worry that he hadn't heard her shout again. He followed the sign down another tunnel, a narrower one with no light at the end, no sprinklers.

Hell, with nothing at the end. The tunnel

simply stopped at a blank wall that looked the same as the walls on either side of him. The wall matched the floor and ceiling, as though he'd gone down a sandy wormhole and run into a dead end.

"Come on, come on!" He cursed under his breath and ran his fingers around the edge, working by the illumination provided by hidden lights, which flickered as though the blast had messed with the power.

There had to be a crack. A latch. Something. The exhibit designers wouldn't have built a tunnel that led nowhere.

Would they?

The lights flickered again and died just as his fingers found a pressure pad. Crouched in the darkness, alone and armed, he held his fingers to the pad and pressed his ear to the blank wall, which *had* to be a door.

At first, he heard nothing. Then he heard the sweetest sound ever. Cassie's voice, giving somebody holy hell.

Then he heard a gunshot.

And his heart stopped.

"YOU WANT TO SAY that again?" Nevada asked. He gestured to the hole blasted in the roof of the kiva, at the powdery, plastery dust raining down.

Cassie's heart drummed against her ribs. "I said that only a wuss would kill because someone else told him to. That's not very original, you know. That's not very—"

"Shut up!" He twisted her arm up higher, until her shoulder screamed with pain and she went limp because it was either that or pass out.

He shoved her to the floor beside the dead woman, not close enough to touch, but near enough that Cassie could see the woman's skin going waxy, to see the cheerful pink polish on her nails and the stump of her severed index finger.

Cassie nearly retched from the pain and the sight, but held it in, held it together.

Barely.

She yanked her eyes up to Nevada and bared her teeth. *Make him mad,* she heard one of her instructors say. *Get him to rush you, then go for his crotch.*

It wasn't Lee in her head now. He was gone. In his place, she'd found the memory of her classes. Her training. Her friends.

The man she loved.

Seth.

"What sort of a pansy goes after women, anyway? Not much of a challenge, if you ask me," she goaded Nevada. *Just a step closer,* she urged him. *Just. One. More. Step.* She'd kick him in the crotch, in the knee, in the stomach, wherever she could reach him.

She wouldn't think about what might happen, what already had. Seth had been buried in the explosion. The bastard on the loudspeaker had switched the audio over to the museum lobby just after the blast. She'd felt the tremors, heard the shouts, and the awful, terrible silence. Then she'd heard her cowork-ers shouting over the echoes of secondary col-lapses. She'd heard her name and Seth's. She'd heard the desperation in the voices, the rapid-fire orders to start digging through the rubble, to find another way through into the Anasazi exhibit.

She'd heard Alissa's voice, sounding stressed. But she'd also heard Mendoza and Piedmont, and half a dozen others she could have sworn hated her.

They were all cursing and urging each other on, not just to find Seth, but to find her.

"They won't get here in time," Nevada said, as though he'd read her mind. "They'll be too late. They always are. Stupid-ass cops." He grabbed her by the throat without warning, and forced her to the ground with more strength than his midsized frame suggested.

She struggled, kicking at him and scratching at those cold, dead eyes.

They were shark's eyes, she thought.

Predator's eyes.

He replaced his choking hand with his shod foot and pressed down on her windpipe hard enough to send skitters of gray dancing across her vision. She gurgled and flailed out, but he had her pinned.

Her heart iced over when he bore down harder on her throat and shifted so he could grab her left hand. He reached across and plucked the bloodstained knife from the floor.

Then he chuckled, flattened her hand against the floor and set the blade against the first joint of her index finger.

"I always like to take a souvenir," he said conversationally as the lights flickered overhead.

And he began to saw.

AT THE SOUND of the gunshot, Seth had hit the button on the wall, intending to barrel through and take out the man on the other side. But when the power kicked back on moments later, the sliding door opened to reveal no room, no man. Instead, he saw the outside of a beehive-shaped structure made of two-by-fours, steel beams and composite.

He'd wound up on the outside of the display somehow.

And Cassie was inside it. He could see the bullet hole punched through the top and hear the muffled sounds of a struggle within.

He wanted to shout her name, to tell her he was coming, but he didn't dare. The bastard had a gun, and Seth had no intention of being a target as he scaled the sloped side of the display.

He would have to be quick and quiet.

There was no other choice.

He holstered his weapon to leave his hands free, and set his foot on the lowest tier of steel beams. He heard voices inside, and wondered what had happened to the third man. His gut kicked a warning, but he didn't know what else to do. He couldn't wait for backup, couldn't take the time to look for the mastermind.

He needed to get to Cassie.

Needed to save her.

He tested the beam, jiggling a moment to see if the structure would sway, or if he would alert the man inside. When there was only a small noise, Seth started up, praying he would be in time.

Praying she'd still be alive when he reached the top.

THE FIRST SLICE was a white fury of pain, of bodily insult and injury. Cassie bucked against Nevada and screamed, almost paralyzed with disbelief that he'd cut her, that this was happening to her. She wasn't supposed to be caught like this. She was a cop for chrissake! She was trained! She was—

Captured. Powerless. She wept as the knife bit deeper into her finger and grated against bone. She screamed again. An unholy light crept into her captor's cold eyes as he fed off her pain.

"That's it," he murmured, "that's the way.

Let it out. Nobody can hear you, he's promised the back exits are blocked. You can scream as loud as you want. Even if they can hear you, they can't get to you. You're all alone."

This time when she screamed, her voice cracked with pain, with the hopelessness. Her mind fragmented away from the weight of his body, the feel of his foot across her throat and the hot sear of the blade severing nerves and tendons. She though about Seth, her lover.

Her love.

He was gone and she'd missed out on telling him she loved him. He might not want to hear it, but she didn't care. She needed him to know.

Seth! she called in her heart, though she knew he was already gone. *Help me!*

And then suddenly there was a light shining above her, a hand reaching down, an angel coming down through the authentic-looking smoke hole in the center of the model kiva—

Only it was no angel. It was Seth.

And the look on his face would have done a demon proud.

HE SAW THE BLOOD first—Cassie's blood spilling too red over the knife, over the man's hand. Her skin was pale and the horrible, wrenching screams had stopped.

Please, God, let me be in time.

He dropped down through the hole and landed square atop Cassie's captor as the bastard reared back and lifted the knife high for the final slash. The man shouted and twisted, slashing high and wild while Seth clamped his legs around his torso and squeezed as hard as he could. The wiry man bucked beneath him and they spun and went down in a sprawl.

Seth slammed into the floor hard and felt his right knee give. Agony howled up his leg and his calf went numb, but he ignored the pain. He staggered to his feet and reached for his holster.

"Seth, look out. He's got a gun!"

Cassie's voice brought a wash of heat and relief, but her message came a split second too late. The man tossed his knife aside and hauled out a gun that looked police-issue. Maybe the one Cassie had lost in the earlier chase after the first murder. Maybe another.

The men faced each other for a heartbeat, weapons pointed at each other's hearts, neither flinching.

The man's average-looking face flattened in an eerily emotionless smile. "Even if you kill me, the planner will still kill you both. He's watching even now. Like an overseer. A god." He raised his voice and called, "Tell him! Tell him that there's no way out, that I'll have my women and my souvenirs, that nobody can take that away from me! Not the slut. Not anybody!"

His only answer was silence.

The man's breathing sounded suddenly harsh in the false circular room. Varitek spared a glance at Cassie. He'd expected her to be curled up in the corner, cradling her wounded hand.

Instead, she was inching her way toward the knife. When she saw his glance, she mouthed, *Distract him, damn it!*

But the madman was already distracted, and becoming more agitated by the moment. "Tell him!" he shouted toward the ceiling. "Tell him that you've got the stupid-ass Bear Claw cops chasing their own tails now, that it's all gone according to your plan!"

When there was still no answer, the gun in the man's hand began to shake. His eyes went wide and white and his lips pulled back across his gums. *"Tell them!"*

"He's gone," Seth said. He kept the gun trained on the other man, but held out a hand. "He left you. You don't have any backup. Give me the weapon. I can help you. I can—"

"You can die!" the madman screamed, and he fired.

Seth saw it coming and threw himself flat,

but there was no place to hide in the round room, no way out except the smoke hole fifteen feet off the ground. He rolled and fired, missed and fired again, catching the other man in the meaty part of the leg with his second shot.

The bullet should have brought the guy down. Instead, pushed past pain by betrayal or insanity or both, the madman twisted his lips in a grimace of disgust, raised his weapon and sighted on Seth. He said, "The plan works both ways. I may not have any backup, but neither do you."

His finger tightened on the trigger and Seth dove for the bastard's legs, braced for the burn of impact, but instead the man screamed and collapsed in an ungraceful heap.

A buck knife protruded from his ankle.

Seth flipped the bastard onto his belly, stripped his belt off and used it to strap his hands and feet together. Once that was done, he leaned close and said, "You're wrong. I had the best backup I could ever ask for." Seth grinned, feeling the first stirring of relief. "I've got Cassie."

WHEN SETH TURNED to her, breathing heavily and looking every inch the arrogant, too-bossy Fed she'd once ordered off her crime scene, Cassie smiled. "You're alive."

He limped over to her, favoring his right leg, looked down at her with those serious green eyes, and touched her cheek. "So are you."

He kissed her, and somehow the words didn't seem so important anymore. She leaned into him, savored the solid strength and the warmth of him, and felt a final tear leak from between her lashes.

He caught it with a kiss. "Finger hurt?"

"Not unless I think about it." Which she was determined not to do. She held her wounded hand tight to her chest and told herself it was numb. Which it was. Mostly. "I'm just…" She trailed off, trying to find the right words. "I thought you were gone. In the explosion." Which reminded her. "The voice! There's a third man, he—"

Seth stopped her with a gentle touch of his fingertip to her lower lip. "I know. He's long gone. I wound up in some sort of access tunnel and found vid screens, microphones, the whole bit. He'd made a decent nest for himself. We'll get some evidence off of it. Later." He eased her to her feet. "Much later. First, it's the hospital for you."

She glanced down and smiled crookedly at his knee. "You, too."

He chuckled. "We're quite a pair, aren't we?"

It seemed wrong to think of love with a woman's discarded body in the corner and an unconscious man bound with his own belt on the floor. But then again, Cassie had never been one to do things by the rules when it came to relationships.

Neither, it appeared, did Seth, because as the

sounds of banging and shouts from outside the sealed door indicated that the Bear Claw cops had found them and were just about through the rubble and the door, Seth leaned down and kissed her again, and then said, "I've been thinking."

She savored the taste of him and the rush of good, solid warmth that battled the rising pain in her arm. "Yeah? Me, too." She slanted a sidelong glance at him. "I'm bad-tempered. Moody. You won't always like me."

He shrugged. "True. But even when I'm ticked off, I'll still love you."

And just like that, he cut the legs right out from underneath her little speech. She stared at him. "Oh."

He cocked an eyebrow. "Is that a good 'oh' or a bad 'oh'?"

"A good one." She closed the distance between them and touched her lips to his. "I love you, too. I'm not quite sure what to do with the feeling yet, but I know it's there. Will you stick with me while I figure it out?"

"We'll stick with each other," he said gruffly, and gathered her close for a longer, wetter, hotter kiss.

They were wrapped together like that when the others broke through. There was an immediate cheer, laced with a good dose of catcalls, but for a change the hoots didn't bother Cassie, because they weren't aimed at her. Not really. Or if they were, they were meant in a good way.

A part-of-the-team way.

As she and Seth were hustled out of the kiva and down to the ambulance, she couldn't help glancing back at the dead woman and the trussed-up figure of the man she'd known simply as Nevada.

Seth met her eyes when she turned back to pick her way through the rubble leading out to the street.

"He's still out there," Seth said, voice sober. "There's still one more. The planner, he called him. The mastermind of this whole twisted plan."

"Yeah." Cassie suppressed a shiver, knowing the city wouldn't be safe until they'd identified and captured the third man. He could be anyone. Anywhere. She had nothing more to go on than a distorted voice and a feeling of malevolence.

But they had the evidence from the vent shaft, she thought, feeling a hint of optimism. She glanced back again and saw Nevada being hustled out in handcuffs. And they had the second man. Maybe they'd learn something from questioning him, maybe from backtracking his movements over the past months.

Maybe.

"We'll manage it," Seth said quietly. He took her hand. "How do you feel about commuting a bit to get to Bear Claw?"

She slanted him a look. "You mean from Denver?"

"Maybe halfway between. A compromise of

sorts. I'll sell my place, you give up yours. It could work." He looked unsettled, a little uncertain, two emotions she never would have expected to associate with Seth Varitek.

And because he looked like she felt, excited and confused at the same time, she grinned. "A compromise. That sounds good."

And it did.